What I

For Shrieking Out Loud! One minute it's chortle-in-the-gut funny! The next so poignant it nudges at the heart! Joyce Faulkner may single-handedly bring the two-minute essay back into vogue. ~ Carolyn Howard-Johnson, author, poet, publicist, teacher. www.CarolynHoward-Johnson.com

Joyce Faulkner's latest book is a quick witted, multi-faceted romp across thirty-something short stories that span topics from dog whispering to the relationship between nightmares and dark horses. I found her well-crafted stories entertaining, poignant, and amusing. I highly recommend *For Shrieking Out Loud!* ~ Raymond Grant, author of *Don't Be Impatient . . . Read a Short Story!* and *Flashes in the Pan, Fifty Short Stories for the Impatient*

One can't help but identify with the pictures Joyce Faulkner paints with her words in *For Shrieking Out Loud!* She is smart and funny; reading this book is like visiting with a very entertaining friend. ~ Carolyn Scott, publisher of "M.D. News," Greater Pittsburgh edition and "All Print Media Custom Publishing and Advertising"

Faulkner takes scenes from life and gives them back to us with humor and an impish grin. ~ Jerry Bolton, author of *fairy!: A Cautionary Tale* and *Mother's Revenge*

Joyce Faulkner's fresh tongue-in-cheek humor turns the grains of sand from the commonality of our lives into delightful pearls. Her Bombeckian style is sure to have Erma smiling! ~ Julie Peters, aspiring poet and columnist

For Shrieking Out Loud! is like *Sex and the City*, without a lot of sex or city . . . funny and thoughtful all at the same time. ~ Anna Marie Gire, editor of "Women's Independent Press"

For Shrieking Out Loud! is a delicious box of chocolate for the soul! This light, breezy and fast-paced read is full of gentle smiles, chuckles and out-loud belly laughs. With titles that entice and intrigue, Joyce reveals the many touching and funny moments of her life with an occasional twist or bawdy moment. Her slices of life out-Bombeck Bombeck. These are more than slices of life. They're the whole damn pie! An entertaining must read! ~Douglas R. Bergman, author of *Names I Can't Remember* (Shelton Award Winner) ISBN 0975917714

For Shrieking Out Loud!, had me laughing out loud at those moments when I realized how I could relate to many of Joyce's stories. Having worked in finance for over thirty years, I read "Roll the Dice and Cross Your Fingers" and found myself saying "your right , Joyce, you are so right." ~ Mary Grace Musuneggi, Wealth Management Consultant, Pittsburgh, PA

Whether it's an Amazon short or a column, novel or nonfiction, I love to read Joyce Faulkner. She makes me laugh. She makes me think. Faulkner deserves best-selling recognition, and I wager she is well on her way to receiving it. ~ Allyn Evans, author of *Grab The Queen Power* and professional speaker

For Shrieking Out Loud!

For Shrieking Out Loud!

by
Joyce Faulkner

Illustrated by
Kathe Gogolewski

Red Engine Press
Key West, FL

Dedication

To my friends and family and the countless strangers who find themselves the subjects of these ruminations.

Acknowledgments

It takes many hands to create a book. Pat McGrath Avery, my writing partner, edited this book - and by doing so, made it much better than it would have been without her keen eye. Kathe Gogolewski, a talented illustrator, raised the quality of this work by adding charm and visual smiles beyond what my words alone could do. I'm lucky to claim both of these ladies as friends. Dominick Miserandino, the publisher of www.theCelebrityCafe.com, gave me free reign for a weekly column. The stories in this book come from the articles I created for "The Weekly Shriek."

Then there are those folks who endured my gentle ribbing with good-natured chuckles. To authors, friends and respected colleagues: Billy Templeton, Eddie Beesley, Lloyd King, Gary Doss, Ken Kreckel, Hodge Wood, Feather Schwartz Foster, Dale 'Sierra' Seawright, Carolyn Howard-Johnson, Connie Gaudette Beesley, Allyn Evans, Dave Grossman, Paula Breaux King, Georgia Richardson and Jerry Pat Bolton, thanks for laughing with me most of the time - and at me on occasion.

Apologies go to my girlfriends Anna Marie Gire, Karen Scott and Helen Jones for enduring the occasional slings and arrows that I sent their way. My sisters Maeva Mayes and Micki Voekel, my parents - the late Bill and Pauline Plummer, my daughter Carmel Faulkner and her husband Wayne Sexton, my daughter-in-law Nora Greer and my son Nate Faulkner - and of course, my husband John Faulkner all took the brunt of my - er - rapier wit. I'm so very sorry. Special thanks to my friend Mike Van Thiel, the owner of SoHo restaurant on the North Shore of Pittsburgh, for letting me mention his establishment in my column from time to time without suing me - yet.

For Shrieking Out Loud

Foreword..iii
Why Women Usually Say No......................................1
Cool Machines...3
Lost.. 8
The Dog Whisperer.. 12
Triumph at the Pump.. 17
The Ball Game.. 21
Scary Corn.. 26
Flipping the Bird...28
Bear With Me...33
The Good, the Bad and the Chubby...................... 41
The World of Don't.. 43
The Last Present..45
I May Not Know Much..49
It's Not About What You've Lost............................55
Beware a Dark Horse!...57
Of Grandmas and Cowboys.................................. 58
Roll the Dice and Cross Your Fingers....................62
Don't Let the Big Bugs Byte?................................ 65
Remember When I Said 70
DNA... 73
Ode to the Odd.. 76
Sexiness and the Wizard..79
Google, Googol and Love.......................................83
The Call of the Hare.. 87
Bubbles...90
Tea and Empathy..94

My Favorite Ghosts...98
eBaying at the Moon...102
Do You Believe in Magic?..105
Nate the Great...109
Heroes..112
Ducks, Peas and Cleavages..119
Hugs...123
Guilt...125
The Phantom of Bob Evans..131
Once Upon a Time 136

Foreword

I don't like writing forewords for people who are funnier than me. It's like committing professional suicide . . . on purpose. I really prefer to say, "Now wasn't that a nice book," using my most condescending royal voice, and then move on. However, when Joyce Faulkner approached me about writing this one, I was so flattered to be included in anything with her name on it, I said "yes" without giving it a second thought. Kinda reminds me of my high school days.

Inside you'll find a compilation of Joyce's thoughts, ponderings, and pontifications of the most unusual kind. I'm amazed at the depth of her talents. She reminds me of a car commercial - she's capable of going from drama to humor in sixty seconds or less. She can pull you into war and have you shed tears for an era and people you weren't even privileged to be a part of, or . . . have you laughing as she explains how to do battle with Mr. Mechanic. How does she do it? If I knew the answer to that she'd be writing the foreword for *my* book.

You'll find stories about her husband and family, her job(s), her friends and/or enemies, food, clothing, phobias (hers and our own), home management or lack thereof, practical jokes, mean people, and don't forget hair; some *wild*, some without, and of course some *high*, commonly known down here in the South as "county-hair." She covers sin as it has never been covered before, taking it out of the closet and into our homes via cable television. She doesn't even bother to spell out the "S" word (S-E-X), she just comes right out and uses it. The woman has no fear.

We should all be grateful for this collection of stories as each one makes us stop and think. Like when she wrote . . .

Do we need labels on our laser printer cartridges that say, "Do not eat toner"? Or to be told that our TV remotes aren't dishwasher safe? . . . I later commented to her, "Not for dishwashers? Who knew?" She gives us plenty of food for thought; or thoughts about food. Combined they're the blend of just-right, extremely satisfying timeless torts that are appealing to all and ready-made for those of us who love to mull life over, think it through a few times, and then cast off the seriousness of it all and settle for laughs. Let's face it; life is much more satisfying when you see it through a humorist's eyes.

A noted card-carrying "think-tiramisu" dessert person, Joyce delights in showing us her own weaknesses for yummy foods, new and improved technical gadgets, and some of my personal favorites - "heroes." She never misses an opportunity to write about the unthinkable that has become for society the "acceptable." She expands on just how absurd the world truly has become by taking a hilarious swipe at politicians living or dead, yet brings balances back into play by showing how kindness still has a voice. In her story, "The Phantom of Bob Evans," a mysterious stranger pays for her meal. Joyce and her friends spend countless hours trying to figure out "who" and the "why" of it all. Using the sage wisdom we've all come to know and expect from her writings, she puts the situation into perspective by saying . . . *What mattered is that in a horn-honking, impatient, frustrating world - someone was good to me - for no real reason. Hallelujah!*

. . . Speaking of kind, you don't want to miss her take on how the world needs more "kind-hearted liars" in "Sexiness and the Wizard." Better known as white lies, they serve us well on some occasions. Her point that some folks think . . . *honesty is a synonym for meanness* . . . is a good read and valuable lesson for our friends, relatives, coworkers, and especially all future mother-in-laws.

It's my firm belief that Joyce Faulkner could make a cool million just writing copy titles. Where does she get this stuff? It is also my contention, and that of the other humorists in the world, that she do so, and give up writing humor all together. Sigh . . .

Whether you're laughing hysterically or rubbing the goose bumps traveling up and down your arms, you're going to love the journey inside. Consider her compilations a primer for stamping out the mundane. Interesting, amusing, and yet so human from the first to the last, I give you a delightful companion in Joyce Faulkner's *Shrieks*.

~ Georgia Richardson, author of *A Funny Thing Happened on the Way to the Throne*, Humorist and Virtual Assistant for "Boomer Women Speak," and "National Association of Baby Boomer Women"

Why Women Usually Say No

I've been getting some pretty weird offers from the online mashers lately. Perhaps there's a full moon - or maybe it's a rash of testosterone poisonings. For example, one fellow popped up on my screen and offered me five thousand dollars to play with my feet - sight unseen.

I said, "Hey man, I'm old enough to be your mother."

He was quiet a moment and then typed, "You aren't my mother, are you?"

No way. My kid doesn't have five dollars, let alone five grand. I had to ask, "There are millions of women online at this moment. Why are you asking me?"

"Old feet are the best," he explained.

Sheesh!

Another guy messaged me a few minutes later. "Wanna go out for a beet?" he asked.

A beet?! All would-be Lotharios should have spell check, if you ask me.

The real show stopper though was the man who sent me an Instant Message saying, "Are you looking for a male slave?"

Intrigued, I answered, "Sure."

Obviously, this wasn't the answer he'd been expecting. "COOL," he said. "I'll do anything you ask. Anything."

1

"Great," I said. "How about painting my deck?"

He logged off.

Some people have no sense of humor.

Cool Machines

I want to drive that," I said to my husband, Johnny, as we drove through a plethora of orange barrels lining a new ramp off I-279 near our house.

"Drive what?" He was focused on something inside his head, I guess. There didn't seem to be any way he could miss the huge piece of road equipment that looked like a cross between a T-Rex and a Sherman tank.

"That!" I pointed.

He sighed. "You always did have a thing for heavy equipment."

It's true. I've always enjoyed exotic vehicles. We have a scrapbook full of pictures of me pretending to steer cruise ships, river barges, air boats, steam engines and the like. I saunter up to the operator of the object of my desire and make friendly with him (For some reason, it's usually a him.) Eventually, I get him to show me how the machine works and that leads to 'the question'.

Most of the time, the answer is "NO."

In another life, I worked in a steel mill for a summer and I was intrigued with the Basic Oxygen Furnace. A cool old man named Foxy operated it. He could look at the flame and tell within ten degrees what the temperature was. Every day, I'd go in to work, put on my white helmet and steel-toed boots, walk out to the control pulpit and sidle up to Foxy.

"Don't give me that look," he'd cackle.

"Aw, c'mon, Foxy. I can do it."

"You get hurt, little girl, we ALL gonna bleed."

"Yeah, yeah, yeah. Like the furnace is going to run amok if I put my hand on the controls."

Foxy chuckled and went back to work.

I used to think that men refused me access to their very cool vehicles because they were afraid that I'd drive them into a wall. Now I think that they just don't want to share - like that boy that lived down the road from me who had a Karmann Ghia. That was a mega-cool car. I could see myself in it - making doughnuts in the field across the street from my house. However, he wouldn't let me anywhere near it unless I'd give him a tongue kiss. His car was a lot more attractive than he was - leading to a moral dilemma of gigantic proportions. In the end, I realized that we shared something important. We liked that car a lot more than we liked each other.

When I was in college, I dated an English professor - the kind who wore leather patches on the elbows of his tweed blazer and sandals with white socks. He drove an old Austin-Healey 100. We spent hours haggling.

"C'mon, Angus. I know how to drive a stick."

He was adamant. "Everything's on the opposite side of the car, what?"

"If you can do it, I can do it."

"But I cut my teeth on 'er," he said.

"What's that got to do with anything? It'll only take me a minute to adjust."

"Not on my dime, dolly."

"My name's Joyce."

"Quite right."

Angus and I never did see eye to eye on anything.

When I worked for the gas company, I cornered a scrawny fellow named Leon who was responsible for backing the truck with the drilling rig into place. I just about had Leon convinced that I could do it - when the big boss pulled up in his white SUV - beeped his horn and gestured.

Leon gasped. "The boss man is gonna can me!"

"Nonsense. He just wants me out of the truck."

I opened the door. The ground was many feet below me. I looked around for hand and toeholds - and started to climb down. Missing the second one from the bottom, I landed on my butt in the grass.

The boss rolled down his window. "Nice try, Joyce."

I got up and dusted off my jeans. "Five more minutes and I'd have driven off with this thing." It was bluster, of course. Someone would have noticed eventually - and come for me.

"You are persistent, I'll give you that much." He rolled up the window and drove off.

"I bet you drove the rig in when you were my age," I grumbled under my breath.

I looked up at Leon. He scooted back into the driver's seat and slammed the door in my face.

"Coward!" I said with no conviction.

Actually, I share the male fascination with big engines, wheels that are taller than me - gears that mesh perfectly. There's something divine in a perfect design.

When we were in Africa, we visited Karen Blixen's coffee farm at the foot of the Ngong Hills - a short drive from Nairobi. The house looked like it did in the movie *Out of Africa* – and the scenery around it made my heart pound with excitement – or maybe that was the altitude. Who knows? All of that - as beautiful as it was - paled before a large piece of equipment of unknown utility parked at the edge of a wood facing a large meadow.

I wandered around it - touching the heavy painted metal, wondering who created it. I imagined some intense engineer with a sexy brain and a lover's passion for beauty. The machine gleamed in the sunshine. I put my forehead against it – and felt the soul of a man long dead - still alive in the inner workings of his creation, which had been rendered inanimate through disuse.

"What are you doing?" Johnny's voice was soft in my ear.

"Communing with the ghost of the guy who made this."

"What's he saying?"

I stood up and sighed. "That I can't drive it."

Lost

Nothing is where I leave it anymore. I think evil elves move my stuff - and then sit back and laugh while I wander around the house looking for whatever it is that's suddenly "lost". I used to blame the kids but they don't live with us anymore. I try to blame my husband, Johnny, once in a while, but we both know that after that unfortunate incident with the discarded paycheck back in the late 1960s, he'd never touch any of my things - regardless of how untidy he considers my sense of being. Back when we had cats, I'd eye them with suspicion whenever one of my possessions turned up missing, but even I know that kitties don't have the wherewithal to put the iron in the refrigerator. So, rather than take responsibility myself, I've settled on evil elves.

Items that I lose with some regularity are: keys, notebooks, pens, Ann Rule's *The Stranger Beside Me*, my left boot, keys, a head of iceberg lettuce, Ann Rule's *Small Sacrifices*, glasses of diet cola, panties (don't ask), my new Ann Rule's *The Stranger Beside Me Revised*, my left sandal, keys, my hair brush (trust me, this is a major catastrophe when this happens), and my left ballet slipper (which is still missing.) I used to lose the phone but in the olden days, I could always find the wire behind the lamp stand and follow it until the phone itself emerged from under a comforter. Then, wireless phones hit the market and I had to wait until the batteries went down and the headset started chirping like a smoke detector. Of course, by then I'd given up on ever finding the headset and would spend an inordinate amount of time trying to figure out which smoke detector was chirping.

Then came cell phones. Over the years, I've lost my cell phone at least a million times. When I still kept a land line, I'd call my cell and follow the ring. Of course, phone mail complicated things by picking up after only four rings - so I'd have to call over and over again - especially when I'd left my cell in either the refrigerator or the car. Now I don't have a land line so I have to send some innocent bystander an Instant Message and ask him/her to call my cell phone. I could log on as someone else and IM myself on my cell - but it only chimes once and it's hard to carry the computer around typing in IMs every few seconds. Of course, I could email the person that I want to call - but then I wouldn't ever find my phone. Johnny suggested that I have my cell surgically implanted behind my ear - but he was kidding. I think.

It's funny how much stuff I've left in the fridge given how there's never any food in there except doggie bags, mustard and half empty-bottles of dill pickles - and given that I never touch doggie bags. I don't even remember going into the kitchen most of the time - but, when whatever I'm looking for fails to show up anywhere else, I give the old ice box a try and bingo, there's my Ann Rule's *The Stranger Beside Me Revised* behind last night's spinach-artichoke dip from SoHo. Go figure.

It's not just my things that disappear into the clutter of my house or car. I lose myself with some regularity too. My most infamous adventure was back in the early 1980s. Johnny was working on our Volvo d'jour. I tapped him on the shoulder and told him that I was going to take a classmate a copy of this week's homework assignments. I knew where I was going when I backed out of our drive. However, I made a wrong turn as I left our street. After twenty minutes of what I

9

thought was circling around our neighborhood, I realized that I didn't recognize any landmarks, that the sun was behind a cloud and that I had no clue which way was north - not that I knew whether home was north or not. That was before I had a cell to lose, so I stopped at a roadside phone booth. When I tried to call home, it was long distance - and of course, I lost my only quarter down a hole in my pocket. You should have heard Johnny's voice when the operator asked him if he'd accept the charges.

You can see why I adapted to computers quickly. First of all, I never once left my computer in the fridge. Secondly, I can use Windows Explorer to find anything on any of my hard drives - and I've not lost any of them except for the thumb drive, but it was in my computer case and not **really** lost. Google won my heart early on - you can find just about anything with it. Now I realize you are thinking that finding things on the Internet isn't like keeping track of your possessions - but it is a quick way to retrieve lost IRS forms, canceled checks from 2004 and replacement copies of Ann Rule's *The Stranger Beside Me Revised*.

I've become so accustomed to a virtual world that I'm frustrated when anyone sends me a hard copy of anything. I know it's going to disappear into the mists and without a version of Google that tracks lost household items, I'm at a loss as to what to do other than go stare at SoHo doggie bags in my fridge. Of course, that's enjoyable in a Zen kind of way - staring into an almost empty electronic box that lights up just for me. Sometimes I forget why I'm there and find myself standing on one foot with my hands folded in front of my chest - contemplating the pickles. It only lasts for a moment. Then my eyes refocus and I see my lost hairbrush in the produce drawer. The rush is incredible. It's like Sir Edmond

Hilary felt when he reached the top of Everest, like Harrison Ford felt when he found the Lost Ark or like Ricky felt when he first saw Lucy.

Then, the moment's over and I wander away idly brushing my hair and mumbling, "What **was** I looking for?"

The Dog Whisperer

What's the deal with all these folks whispering to domesticated critters?" I asked my girlfriends as we had lunch at SoHo the other day. "First it was horses, now it's dogs. What's next goldfish? Cats?"

"What's she talking about now?" Anna Marie whispered behind her hand to Karen.

"She's fascinated with Cesar Milan," Karen shrugged. "You know, the Dog Whisperer on TV?"

Anna Marie was under-whelmed. "Wow," she said as she stirred her iced tea. "What does he say to them?"

"That's just it, he doesn't REALLY whisper to them," I explained. "In fact, he doesn't talk to them at all. He just walks them and jerks their leashes and hisses at them."

"Doesn't sound like that big of a deal to me." Anna Marie was still unimpressed. "What's the use of whispering if you don't have a secret?"

"I think Cesar is hot," Karen said. "It's worth watching the show just to see him roller blading with the pack."

"He what?" Clearly, Anna Marie needed to tune in - and soon.

"He's the leader of the pack," I said. "Of dogs."

"Ah. I see."

A child in the back of the restaurant squealed.

"No really. He's got this deal going where he gets into the heads of the dogs. He's got a Dog Psychology Center and everything. He understands how they think and after he rehabilitates them they do what he wants them to."

"Sounds like a useful skill."

The little boy behind us bawled louder.

Karen shuddered. "They need to get that kid out of here.

"Maybe we need a Kid Whisperer," I laughed. "Someone should walk up to him and hiss and point."

"I'm not sure I'm getting an accurate picture here," Anna Marie interjected. "What does this pack person point at?"

I looked at Karen. She shrugged.

"Um - you know, I don't know what he points at," I said.

"The air, I think." Karen added, tentatively.

"And just by hissing and pointing, the dog will stop doing whatever irritating thing it's doing?"

"Yeah, it'll roll over on its back and let you rub its belly."

The shrieks coming from the table behind us got louder.

Anna Marie turned to peer around the edge of our booth. "Having that kid roll over on his back and let me rub his belly isn't exactly what I had in mind."

"Well, you have to do it with authority," I lectured. "You aren't supposed to be angry. You want to show them that you are the dominant one by projecting calm and assertive energy. He says they don't respond to emotion or negotiations like we do."

The beleaguered mother picked up her wailing offspring and headed toward the door.

"Authority, you say?"

"Like this." I poked Anna Marie's upper arm with two fingers. "And then he goes 'TSSSSSST!'"

Anna Marie jumped and scowled, but the screaming kid passing by us in his mother's arms, quieted.

The three of us sat in shocked silence for a second and then said in unison, "COOL."

"Ooooh, Cesar!" Karen hooted.

"This is an incredible tool," Anna Marie exclaimed. "Just think of the possibilities!"

"You think it would work with a man?" Karen asked.

We stared at each other in amused silence.

"A man whisperer?" Anna Marie's voice was hoarse with excitement.

"Might need a bit more leash jerking with men," Karen posited.

"Nope. Just project calm and assertive dominance." I maintained.

"You think it's that easy?"

"Sure."

"Show me." Anna Marie never accepts my theories right out of the box.

We looked around the restaurant. A good-looking young waiter was busing a table a few feet away. Anna Marie and Karen turned back to me with expectant smiles.

14

"Greg?"

"Why not? He's a man."

"Give me a second to warm up." I popped my knuckles, squared my shoulders and took a deep breath.

"Sheesh, you're winding up like Ebby Calvin 'Nuke' LaLoosh in *Bull Durham*," Anna Marie sighed. "Just DO it."

"I will, I will. You don't get calm assertive dominance out of thin air, you know."

"DO it," they both breathed.

"Okay. Here goes."

Our eyes returned to Greg who was absorbed in his work.

I jabbed two fingers into the air. "TSSSSSSSSSST!"

Greg looked up, smiled - and hurried over to our table. "You all need another drink?"

We stared at him in astonishment.

"Uh - sure," Karen bit her lip to keep from giggling. "Bailey's?"

"Tea?" Anna Marie lifted her glass.

Greg looked into my eyes.

"Bailey's is good." It was a whisper.

"This is GREAT!" Karen turned in her seat to watch Greg walk away. "To think, the way to get a man to obey is to treat him like a dog."

"Now, now," Anna Marie laughed. "A nice tip works just as well in a restaurant."

"Hmmm. Perhaps you are right. Maybe we need a different guinea pig."

"I don't dare," Karen said. "I'm a newly wed."

Anna Marie shook her head. "They already KNOW they have to obey me. I was born tall."

Again, they turned to me.

"Cowards," I sighed.

That night, as I climbed into bed, I said to Johnny. "Have you ever seen The Dog Whisperer?"

"You don't like dogs."

"It's not that I don't like them, I'm scared of them."

"Then why do you want a dog?"

"I didn't say I wanted a dog."

"Good." He turned out the lights and rolled over.

"TSSSSSSSST!"

"Nice try," he mumbled before he went to sleep.

Maybe jerking the leash does work better with husbands.

Triumph at the Pump

Look at that," my husband said as we approached a service station on the way to Coldstone Creamery the other day. A young man was walking across the driveway with a ladder. "He's going to change the price."

"Hold on," I said. "Maybe I can make it."

Johnny braced himself. I swerved around a burly Harley biker and accelerated toward the station.

"It's too late," Johnny shrieked. "He's under the sign."

I focused on the road ahead - maybe a quarter mile to go. "No, I can do it. Watch me." The Acura's engine roared and the speedometer crept past seventy.

Johnny's eyes bulged from their sockets. "Look out! We have company at nine o'clock."

In the lane beside me, a blue-haired lady in a matching blue Hummer saw what was about to happen too. She was determined to beat me to the pump.

"I got her, don't worry." I reassured Johnny.

He tightened his seatbelt. "She's got more horsepower."

"I've got more guts."

Up ahead, the service station operator opened his ladder. The septuagenarian beside me sped up. I sped up. A vortex opened up ahead – a tunnel of vibrating energy leading to the driveway under the Exxon sign.

I glanced at Johnny as we approached the final curve. The G-forces pressed him into the passenger seat and smoothed the laugh lines around his eyes. I peeked at my competitor on the left. The wind had blown the curls out of her perm and her lips quivered in a wide chimpanzee-like grin.

We were bumper to bumper when a leaf blew across the road. She stood on her brakes and the rear of the Hummer fishtailed. The break in her forward momentum gave me the opportunity I needed - and I reached the beckoning abyss first. The vortex sucked me in and spit me out. The Acura slid into the driveway just as the service station manager removed the eight from the $2.89 sign.

"It's too late, it's too late." Johnny sobbed as he jumped out of the door and ran around the back of the car.

"It depends on whether he changed the pump price before he changed the sign." I popped the fuel door just as the service station manager moved the nine from the hundred's position to the ten's position.

"Hurry," I begged Johnny under my breath. "Hurry!"

I felt a jolt as Johnny inserted the nozzle into the Acura.

The man rehung the eight.

"$2.98!" I screamed as the pump began clicking away in time with my own beating heart. "Did we make it?"

"We made it!" Johnny thumped the roof of the Acura.

"Nine cents." I collapsed against the seat in relief.

The man jumped down off the ladder and headed back inside the station. The blue Hummer screeched in behind me.

Johnny finished refueling the Acura and replaced the nozzle. As soon as he did, the digital readout on the pump flickered. In my rear view mirror, I watched the woman beat on her steering wheel as the price per gallon became $2.98.

I smiled at her, reveling in my victory.

She scowled back.

"Well, what's her problem?" I asked as Johnny got back into the car.

"She's in a truck. Nine cents a gallon for forty gallons."

"She needn't be so cranky about it. That's what? $3.60 difference? Big woo!"

"She could have had an extra Happy Meal at Mickey Ds if she beat you to the draw."

"Hmmpft!" I said, "It's a dog-eat-dog world." I put the Acura in gear and we continued on our way to Coldstone Creamery.

I dipped my spoon into my sweet cream and chocolate chips. "So how much did we save by winning that race?"

"$1.08." Johnny sucked down his banana shake.

"So how much was my ice cream?"

"$3.50."

"Hm. So I nearly killed us for roughly one-third of a Coldstone Creamery ice cream?"

"Yep."

"Cool."

The Ball Game

The broad-shouldered man stood in our foyer with his baseball cap in his hands.

"I don't think he'd be interested."

"Interested in what?" My husband called from his recliner.

"Playing baseball. I told him you weren't much of an athlete," I said over my shoulder.

"What kind of baseball?" Johnny padded into the foyer barefoot, standing behind me with a bottle of beer in his hand.

"Hello, John." The coach reached around me to shake Johnny's hand. "Softball. After the kids' last game, they can enjoy watching their dads play a few innings."

"That sounds like fun. I'll be there."

I stared at Johnny in surprise. We'd been married twelve years. In all that time, I never saw him play baseball. He was a scholarly soul - a couch potato with soft hands and soft eyes. He stuck his tongue out at me and laughed.

"See you on Saturday." The coach backed out of the door and headed up the street.

"You are going to play ball?" I raised an eyebrow.

"Why not?" Johnny looked offended.

"I didn't know you could play."

21

"I can play." He went back into the living room and the volume on the TV went up.

"Right."

Saturday was hot and sunny. The mothers set up lunch on a long picnic table under a shady tree while the kids finished their season. Dusty and flushed after the last pitch, they threw down their gloves and bats and ran to get chilled bottles of soda pop and hot dogs. I wiped my son's face with a damp cloth and re-braided my daughter's tangled hair. We crawled over the bleachers and settled down with our lunches to watch the dads play.

"I didn't know Daddy could play ball," Carmel said.

"Daddy can play." Nate assured her as Johnny trotted out onto the field wearing a red and white t-shirt and waving to us with a glove on his hand.

I had my doubts. What if he broke his leg? What if he got hit by the ball? What if he had a heart attack? I watched him take his position in center field. He WAS cute all decked out that way. I waved at him and he blew me a kiss as the game began.

The first batter hit a high pop fly to the pitcher who caught it easily. The second man up hit a line drive out to center field. I heard the 'THWUMP' as it landed in Johnny's glove. "Yeah!" I called through my hands and the kids clapped. Johnny tossed the ball back to the pitcher.

"See, Daddy can play!" Nate elbowed his sister in his best 'I told you so' voice.

Johnny crouched. The next batter lofted the ball high over the head of the shortstop and Johnny caught it at his shoelaces.

"WOOOOOO!" I hooted. Carmel whistled through her fingers.

During the next few innings, Johnny proved to be a marvelous fielder - leaping into the air like an antelope, rolling on the grass to pick up ground balls, backing up against the fence to deny the other team a home run. He could hit too. He planted his feet in the dust and gave the bat a couple of practice swings. Looking over his shoulder to see if we were watching, he wiggled his butt. We giggled and hollered, creating a wave among the three of us.

"Sit right here," I told the kids at the end of the fourth inning.

Clattering down the bleachers, I dug a bottle of Coke out of the bottom of the icy barrel and carried it with me to the fence. "Hey, good looking", I called.

Johnny strutted over to the fence and I offered him a sip of the Coke. "Thanks, baby." He tweaked my nose and winked before sucking down half the bottle.

"You're fantastic."

"You're not bad yourself." He handed me the bottle and picked up his glove, turning to catch my eye as he returned to the outfield.

I went back to the kids and the game continued. There was a close call as Johnny and the left fielder nearly collided over a ball that bounced into the air and ended up in Johnny's glove. There were two more hits - one of them a run batted in, the other a double. In the end, Johnny saved the game by getting the final out. The other fathers lined up to slap his hands in a string of jubilant high-fives.

Carmel and Nate ran out onto the field to wrap themselves around each of Johnny's legs as he was presented with a white baseball cap with two-inch letters proclaiming him to be the 'MVP'. I stood by the fence, my hands clasped over my heart watching him laugh and joke with our neighbors. I couldn't identify what I was feeling. Pride? A little, but I was more proud of his talents as an engineer. Happy for his success. Most definitely - but there was something else that I couldn't quite pinpoint.

"He's a hell of a player." A woman with big hair told me.

"Yeah, he is," I agreed with a smile.

"I didn't know he was a jock." A moment later, the coach's wife patted my back as she packed up the food.

"I didn't either."

The kids released Johnny to go play with their friends. Johnny came over to the fence. His nose was sunburned but his eyes glowed. He was brawny and male and sexy. That was it, I realized. I was aware of his physicality and excited by it. "Hey, big boy!" I flirted.

"Take me home," he whispered.

"You got it," I caressed his bristling jaw.

"That's not what I mean."

"Oh?"

He gritted his teeth. "I can't move."

At first, I thought he was kidding. Then I realized that the glow in his eyes was pain-induced. "Sure, baby. Let's get going."

Joyce Faulkner

I gathered up the kids and we started down the hill to our house. He leaned on me and walked in a stiff-legged shuffle. At home, I got the kids settled in front of the TV and went upstairs to run Johnny a hot bath. He sprawled on the bed in his dusty clothes, staring at the ceiling.

"You were wonderful, honey." I knelt beside him and kissed his cheek.

"Good. Don't make me prove it again."

"No. No, I won't," I whispered as I helped him into the tub.

Scary Corn

I'm scared of cornfields. Now you may think I'm on the odd side, but I maintain that I'm not the only one with this particular phobia. Check out the movies. Some of the scariest scenes ever filmed take place in cornfields. Remember those freaky raccoons stealing half-ripe cobs in *Old Yeller*? Remember that evil crop-dusting plane chasing Cary Grant through the stalks in *North by Northwest*? How about those big apes on horseback pursuing a bunch of naked people and an astronaut or two through a field of maize in the original *Planet of the Apes*? I don't guess they were REALLY naked - I just remember it that way in my nightmares.

There were half a dozen sequels to *Children of the Corn* - if they weren't terrifying, they were at least corny. Then, there were those big-eyed aliens in Mel Gibson's corn in *Signs* - and horror of horror, baseball players in Kevin Costner's *Field of Dreams*. I nearly choked on my popcorn over that one.

The Twilight Zone had an episode where a little boy named Anthony wished anyone who wasn't very, very nice to him out into a cornfield. There was no indication of exactly what happened to the 'un-nice' but I just knew it had to be something bad. Shudder.

Anyway, to capitalize on our national love/hate relationship with corn, farmers have begun setting up cams so that we can watch it grow from the safety of our computers. If you are bored and brave at the same time, other agricultural entrepreneurs have planted their crops into a maize maze that plays on a combination of fears raised by *Signs* and *The Shining*. Imagine running like a rat in endless confusion down a path lined on all sides with that most frightening of leafy plants. Yikes!

They are going to be growing even more corn to create ethanol to reduce our foreign oil consumption. I can see it now - they'll start by plowing under all the tobacco fields. Then they'll do away with tomatoes and beans and watermelons and zucchinis. Then flower gardens will turn corny. Before long, our neighborhoods will be stalked by this beastly grain - and our children will be sucked into . . . okay, so maybe it's time I go take a Valium.

Flipping the Bird

When I was eight, a boy on the playground told Sister Mary Wilhelmina that Johnny Brown (names have been changed to protect the guilty and because I can no longer remember them) had flipped him the bird. Horrified, I imagined a little brown sparrow being tossed tail over beak from one child to another.

When I was ten, a man in a beat up 1948 Ford beeped his horn and swerved around us as we were driving down Towson Avenue. "Look at that," my dad snorted. "He tossed me the bird." Now, I'm not stupid. I knew it wasn't the same bird that Johnny Brown had flipped two years before – but I couldn't figure out where these guys were getting all these birds. I spent a lot of time one summer trying to catch a little hummer zipping around the morning glories on our front porch – and I can testify to avian agility and elusiveness. Of course, that explained why the bird tossed by the unhappy driver was nowhere to be seen. My dad must have missed the toss and the feathery lil sucker had flown away.

When I was thirteen, I joined the pep squad for an hour and twenty-three minutes. It's not that I wasn't peppy. I couldn't understand why anyone would want to spell out "Go Buffaloes" by holding up blue and white pieces of cardboard - and why if we did it well, our efforts would make football players play better. Besides doing anything in unison had become burdensome for me by that time. Anyway, our first event was a float ride down Garrison Avenue in our cute little uniforms. As we approached

Immaculate Conception Church, we passed a farmer loading a big sack of something smelly into the back of his truck. We went into our act about that time, cheering and shaking our pom-poms. He scowled and showed us his middle finger. I was shocked. Clearly this guy didn't find us as adorable as we presumed ourselves to be - and even though I'd never seen that gesture before, there was no mistaking its rude meaning. "Did you see what that man did?" The girl next to me pointed at the unrepentant culprit who'd already gotten in his pickup and was backing away from the curb. "Never mind," Sister Mary Wilhelmina clapped her hands and started the next cheer. The other members of the team joined her, but I was busy pondering why a perfect stranger would be so mean to a bunch of giggling little girls. It wouldn't be the last time a snarling face spoiled a good time for me.

A couple years later, a young man clued me in on the true meaning of the gesture. However, no one seemed to know why extending the middle finger was called "flipping the bird."

"It's phallic," one of my more precocious friends explained. "And they call male genitalia a bird."

Hmm.

"What kind of bird?" I asked.

"Oh, Joyce." She shook her head and powdered her nose as though that answered my question - then she stopped for a minute. "A swan maybe? Or an ostrich?"

I envisaged a man with a long white-feathered appendage with a beak at the end. "I don't see it," I said finally. "It doesn't seem practical. Seems to me if it's anything it should be a snake."

"Flipping a snake doesn't sound right," she said.

"Would probably break its neck," I agreed.

"Would be hard on a bird too," she observed.

"Technically, you aren't flipping anything," I pointed out. "It's more like you are jabbing."

"And it's only your finger," she conceded.

"Maybe it's like that saying, that the darkest clouds have a silver lining."

She dropped her powder puff. "What?"

"You know, like God gives us rain to make us appreciate the sun?"

"What's that got to do with giving anyone the finger?"

"You use your thumb for hitching a ride and thumbing your nose, right?"

She squinted.

"And you use your index finger to point."

"Okay?"

"Your ring finger is for rings."

She brightened. "Yeah."

"Your pinkie is what babies hold onto."

"What's any of this got to do with flipping someone the bird?"

"Well," I said. "What's the purpose of your middle finger?"

She stared at her hand, wiggling first the right middle finger and then the left. "I don't know."

"That's about all it does, right?"

I could see that the thought upset her. "I sometimes use it to scratch my nose," she said hopefully.

"No, you don't."

"No, I don't." She sighed. "So how's that like the silver lining in clouds?"

"Don't you see? The only thing we use that finger for is to express our disdain for someone. We use it to be mean."

"And?"

"So God puts irritating people in our path so that our middle fingers have a function."

She stared at me with her mouth open.

"Think about it," I said. "If there were fewer jerks in the world, we'd only have four fingers."

It made sense at the time.

Bear With Me

There's nothing like camping to make you appreciate a Holiday Inn. Even the funky lamps glued to the nightstands seem the height of luxury after dealing with Coleman lanterns and key chain flashlights. Oh, the joy of Denny's chili cheese omelets at two o'clock in the morning - but I digress. I wanted to tell you the story of our trip to a KOA campground back in the early 1980s when Johnny and I were young and everything seemed to be a marvelous adventure.

We packed our Volvo station wagon to the roof with a two-room tent, camping equipment, several cases of champagne, two coolers of frozen food and boxes of plastic cups and paper plates. Our friends Grace and Jim followed in their tiny Pontiac Sunbird, the hatch filled with a two burner camp stove, cartons of cooking utensils and bag after bag of groceries. We were loaded for bear.

The sun was setting as we pulled into the campsite. It was in a shady glade not too far from a babbling brook. Everyone went to work unloading the cars. Within fifteen minutes, Johnny was pounding tent stakes into the ground and Jim was building a fire inside a ring of painted rocks. Grace and I unpacked our guitars and a case of champagne before declaring ourselves off duty and popping the first cork. It was almost dark when the bear came over the ridge.

"Honey, look. There's a bear." Grace was sitting in a lawn chair with her feet up on the picnic table bench.

"What?" Jim was on his hands and knees, holding a Zippo against the edge of an artificial log he'd bought at the Giant Eagle.

"A bear!"

We all followed her quivering pointed index finger. It was a huge black beast with a silver tag in his ear. He stared at us for a moment before lumbering across the campsite toward where Grace and I sat. "A BEAR!" She screamed and fell over backwards in the lawn chair. Startled, the bear changed directions, waded across the babbling brook and disappeared into the woods.

Jim, Johnny and I found Grace cringing behind the Sunbird. "More than you could 'bear'?" Jim didn't smile.

"I wish I had my Kodiak camera." Johnny elbowed me.

The alarm on Grace's face melted into annoyance. "Oh you, guys!" Grimacing over a broken fingernail, she poured herself another Asti Spumante.

"He was as tame as a pussy cat, didn't even 'bear' his teeth." Jim stripped the leaves off of a small branch with a penknife.

"Ha, ha!" Grace sipped her drink.

"Why did he have that thing on his ear?" I asked.

"There are a lot of bears in the area. They all look alike. The rangers tag them so that they know which is which." Johnny gave a quick tug on a line and the pop-up tent popped up.

"That one 'bears' a strong resemblance to my boss." Jim ducked as Grace tossed a marshmallow at him. "I'd recognize him a mile away."

"You think it'll come back?" It was dark now and the campfire didn't make much light. Grace moved her lawn chair out of the shadows.

Johnny threw our sleeping rolls into the tent. "That was a pretty big bear. Probably got claws like straight razors. The only thing between him and us is aluminum and nylon."

Grace glanced over her shoulder into the woods. She wasn't sure if Johnny was kidding or not.

"Ahck! Bu-bu-bu-bahk!" Jim put his hands under his armpits and flapped his elbows like a chicken.

"Uh huh. I see how it is. Well, I'm sleeping with the car keys around my finger just in case I have to make a quick exit."

🐻 🐻 🐻

The plan called for each couple to take turns cooking. Johnny and I provided hot dogs, macaroni salad and s'mores the first night along with a strange concoction of cranberry juice, triple sec and champagne. Grace scrambled eggs for breakfast the next morning and Jim served us Grand Mimosas. I made tuna salad sandwiches for our trip to a small island in the middle of the lake. We ate it on the beach with strawberries and champagne.

Jim was a gourmet cook and dinner was on him. He'd planned this meal since we first decided to go camping - filet mignon wrapped in bacon, Caesar salad, baked potatoes with sour cream and chives, chocolate cake - more champagne. The rest of us would have been happy with onion dip and Fritos, but Jim was determined and set to work right away.

"You want help?" Two days of drinking made my offer half-hearted.

"No, you go play guitar with Grace." He shooed me away.

"Fine." My fingers were too rubbery to play so I staggered into the tent and stretched out.

I awoke to the smell of roasting potatoes and crawled out of the tent with a pounding headache. Johnny was sprawled across the picnic table holding a can of beer on his forehead. Grace was in her lawn chair, her head thrown back - an empty bottle of sparkling chardonnay in the grass beside her.

Jim on the other hand was in a great mood. He'd set the Coleman stove on a large rock and was humming as he whipped up some kind of sauce. The smell was wonderful - and nauseating.

I staggered up to him. "Aspirin."

"What?" He was as sober as a judge and as happy a camper as I'd ever seen.

"Aspirin?"

"In the medicine box. Johnny put it in the back of the Volvo." He jerked a thumb over his shoulder.

I found the precious white tablets and tossed them down with the only liquid available - the dregs of Johnny's beer.

"What's going on," Johnny grunted at me without taking his hand from over his eyes.

"Dinner in the works." I whispered as the aspirin and beer mixed with the champagne in my belly.

"OH, NO."

"Oh, yes." I sat down on the bench beside him.

"I better go to the head then." He rolled off the table and belched.

"I think it's called a john in the KOA by-laws." I called after him.

He wandered over to where Jim was slicing anchovies on his natural sandstone counter. He swayed and hiccuped as Jim elaborated about the delightful menu to be. Always polite, Johnny clapped Jim on the back before stumbling off to find the bathroom - or whatever you call it in the woods.

Grace sat up. "Honey, the bear's back. Why don't you get out the camera and take its picture?" She hadn't lost her fear. She just wasn't going to give us fodder for more bear jokes.

Jim continued cooking, unaware of our visitor.

The bear ambled toward us, following the exact same path as the night before.

"Jim, get the camera." Her voice was louder.

"What?" He wrapped raw bacon around our filets.

The bear observed us with bored eyes before heading toward the babbling brook.

"He's getting away." Grace stamped her foot.

Jim was absorbed in securing the bacon with toothpicks. "What's getting away?"

"JIM! Get the camera!"

"The what?" Jim turned around as the bear splashed across the stream.

"He's gone now," I said as though the issue was resolved.

"NO!" Grace put her fingers in her mouth. "WHEEEEEWWWWWWW!" The whistle was shrill and loud. Birds lifted into the air over their roosts and crickets stopped chirping.

The bear's ears perked. As it turned to check out the source of that horrendous sound, it caught the smell of filet mignon sizzling in the hot skillet. Snorting, it put its head down and headed back into camp - fast.

Jim's eyes widened. "Grace, get in the car."

The bear was between Grace and me sitting at the picnic table and Jim standing by the big rock. We stood up. It made a snuffling sound and kept coming. Jim ducked one way, then the other before bolting for a young oak. Grace and I waited another beat before we turned and ran. The back of the Volvo was open. I'd neglected to close it after my aspirin quest. We piled in and closed the hatch behind us. Fighting through the boxes, we climbed over the back seat so we could see out through the windshield.

Jim cowered behind the sapling. The bear ignored him and made straight for the food. Jim dodged from tree to tree bellowing in frustration as the beast found his long-planned and carefully executed gourmet dinner spread on top of the rock. It rose up on its hind legs and put one paw on either side of the Coleman stove. The four filets wrapped in bacon went down first. While the bear leaned back its head and pumped its massive jaws, Jim hurried to the Sunbird and crawled inside. We waved to him from the Volvo. He frowned - and we turned back to watch the bear as it found the Caesar salad with fresh-grated cheese, raw eggs and thinly sliced anchovies mixed with tender romaine lettuce. A dish of sour cream didn't last beyond one long lick from its enormous tongue. It batted the baked potatoes in their tin foil jackets around until they broke open.

That's when Johnny came back from the bathroom.

Unsteady on his feet as he crossed the small white bridge over the babbling brook, he found his way to the rock and stood beside the bear as it rolled hot potatoes under its paws. It took Johnny a minute to realize that the big furry form beside him wasn't Jim. Slowly, he turned his head and looked up at the bear towering over him.

I screamed, "Get out of there, Johnny," but we had rolled up all the windows on the Volvo and my shriek was muffled.

Johnny waved both arms in an abrupt half circle. "SHOO!"

The bear staggered backwards on its hind legs before dropping to all fours and galloping off into the woods.

I crawled out of the Volvo and ran to Johnny. "Are you crazy? He could have killed you." I threw my arms around him, sobbing with relief.

"Aw, he wasn't going to hurt me. He'd had dinner." Johnny peeled my fingers from around his neck and reached down to pick up tiny bits of tin foil from the shredded potatoes.

Jim and Grace approached hand in hand. Everything was gone or ruined. A bottle of cooking wine lay shattered at our feet. The oily skillet was smoking.

"He even ate the jimmies off the chocolate cake." Jim was crestfallen.

"It smelled wonderful, honey." Grace tried to console him.

"Sure did, buddy." Johnny gathered up the aluminum salad bowl. It was empty save for the lick-marks in the bottom.

"What are we going to do now?" I flicked a piece of bacon fat off the side of the rock. All that was left of the steaks were the broken bits of toothpick.

"There's nothing but day-old macaroni salad." Jim held up a torn bag of crushed potato chips.

My stomach rolled. "I'm not eating THAT again."

"I'm not spending the night in a tent with that thing wandering around out there." Grace crossed her arms over her chest and stuck out her lower lip.

The four of us turned and gazed into the woods on the other side of the babbling brook. A loud crack! Something moved deep in the brush.

We left them at the crossroads. They turned toward Pittsburgh. We chose the Holiday Inn and Denny's - and that's the story. It's all perfectly true. I swear. Well, except for the part about the jimmies - I sneaked them myself when Jim's back was turned.

The Good, the Bad and the Chubby

Let's talk about one of my favorite subjects - sin. My Aunt Pete used to define it as anything that's illegal, immoral or fattening. I concur - especially about the fattening part. A delicate dish of tiramisu is so titillating that it MUST be evil. We Americans are like that - endlessly suspicious about the good things in life. Take sex. We can't help but titter about it because we know that somewhere, someone (probably a parental unit) is shaking her head and tsk-tsk-tsking. We are much more accepting of our baser instincts now than we were in the 1960s though. When I started college, women were not allowed to wear slacks on campus unless we ALSO wore a raincoat - even when it wasn't raining. That's because if men caught sight of our thighs, they would be so aroused that they couldn't control themselves and might run amok. I submit that this was before tiramisu was so popular and women's thighs hadn't plumped up like frankfurters in a microwave. There WAS a lot of amok running in those days, but there's no proof it had anything to do with whether coeds wore slickers over their knickers. Things are different now. Sin has moved out of the shadows and is featured each week on cable television.

I learned about sin from the nuns - and boy, do they know a lot about it. If one is motivated, there is a nice variety of peccadilloes available. We inherited original sin from Adam and Eve. It hardly seems fair to handicap a baby that way, but there you have it. Now that scientists have mapped the human genome, I trust that they've identified the guilty strand of DNA and are busy developing a virus to deal with it once and for all. Venial sins are the ones you have to mention in the confessional, but they are not all that bad in the major scheme of things - taking one egg out of the dozen, boiling it and putting it back into the carton just to see your mother freak out when she wants to fry eggs is an example of that one. Mortal sin is major. You don't want to get caught dead with one of those suckers in your column. However, common opinion about what constitutes this ultimate evil varies depending on your political persuasion. Being an activist judge counts if you are a Republican, while Democrats point the finger at greedy corporate CEOs. Anti-abortionists focus on one particular act, while Muslims have a multi-page list. Some people think gambling is wicked - unless, of course, they win. Others reserve the really big sins for lying and/or sexual perversion. A friend of mine is sure that drilling in Alaska is the ultimate wrongdoing. My husband thinks banking fees are the devil's handiwork.

You see, sin's all about what's in the head of the sinner. My dad thought for sure I was going straight to hell the first time I appeared at the breakfast table in mascara. I, on the other hand, was willing to risk eternal damnation if only Ronnie Coleman would notice me. Other people's foibles are both amusing and inexplicable. That's why you see so many little old ladies at the check out stand perusing "The National Inquirer" or "The Globe" or "The Star." The sins of Marilyn and Elvis and Di continue to shock and intrigue day in and day out. Knowing that space aliens have sexual appetites is both reassuring and alarming. As a nation, we are mesmerized by wrongdoing. That's why Nancy Grace is so popular. She expresses just the right amount of fascination and horror, condemnation and glee - she's so one of us that we can't help but love her. That woman knows sin almost as well as the nuns. Hallelujah!

The World of Don't

Did you ever notice how hard it is to get through the day without breaking a law? Even if you aren't a celebrity like Michael or Robert or OJ, it's tough. There are so many prohibitions out there that you can't move without stepping over a line somewhere. There are the laws of nature, physics, mathematics and attraction. There are moral codes, housing codes, color codes and area codes. We have to abide by the rules of evidence, etiquette, spelling and order. Agencies, commissions and homeowners associations govern our property rights. We have to get licenses if we want to drive cars, sell booze, catch fish, get married or buy guns. On top of all that, we have a nice assortment of accords, treaties, pacts and agreements that further limit our options.

If it were only state, local and federal mandates, life would be easy. Don't want me to leave my Acura next to a fire hydrant? No biggie. The parking garage only charges eighteen bucks a day. I shouldn't stuff a three-pound rump roast down the front of my Levis? Fine. I'll fish it out and pay the checkout girl. Don't carry eyebrow tweezers in my carry-on bag when I go through security at the airport? Sure. Take them. I can buy more when I get to where I'm going.

I can handle all of that easily. It's the other dictates that get to me. You know the ones that spoil a good time? Don't slather French's Mustard on Saltine Crackers. Don't kick the dentist and scream no matter WHAT he's doing to you. Redheads can't wear red. Don't pull the fire alarm in your big sister's dorm just to see what will happen. Every kitchen has to have an oven. Women can't drive stick shifts. Don't kiss and tell. I mean, really – telling is half the fun.

These little intrusions into our lives start the moment that we can do more than just lay in our mothers' arms and coo. Remember how they wouldn't let us stick our fingers in the light socket? Or poke beans up our noses? Remember when we couldn't date that good-looking boy because he drove a VW bus and everyone knew that boys who drove VW buses were hippies, and hippies were dope fiends, and if we dated dope fiends we'd become dope fiends too? There was this great big wonderful world out there and they wouldn't let us touch it for fear we'd get hurt. That was a good thing when we were kids - but hey, now we are adults. Right?

Wrong. Someone is still trying to protect us from ourselves, it seems. It's nice of them of course, but I'm not sure it's necessary. "Don't pick up your lawnmower to trim the tops of your hedges" or "Don't put your dog in the microwave to dry him off after a bath" seem obvious to me. Do we need labels on our laser printer cartridges that say, "Do not eat toner"? Or to be told that our TV remotes aren't dishwasher safe? I can dig that manufacturers want to be SURE that we understand those little product features - but I have an advanced degree, ya know?

The reasons behind some rules still confuse me. Have a lot of people been eating their wrinkle cream? Are the hospitals filling up with folks who tried to dry their hair in the shower? What's the story with those "Watch out for aggressive drivers" signs along the highways? Do escaped mental patients likely to be overcome with road rage frequent the same stretch of the highway so often that we need to be warned about them? I wonder about things like that while putting paper clips in my ears and munching on buttons.

The Last Present

Ever notice that some folks really know how to give a gift and others don't have a clue? My parents were pretty good at it - but not spectacular. They gave me what I wanted. Simple. Uninspired. Loving. I proudly wore my coveted socks with blue lace, built imaginative structures with Tinker toys and filled an armoire with 'Little Golden Books'. My paternal grandmother's presents were weird - things like Styrofoam angels decorated with sequins and fuzzy feathers or long necked dolls made out of wire coat hangers. They were for looking at and not for touching, she explained when I opened them. I was supposed to say thank you and then my mother put them away where I couldn't 'mess them up'. When I left home, I had seventeen years of crafty little untouchables stored in my closet.

However, my maternal grandfather was a whole 'nother ballgame when it came to presents. Papa seemed to sense the essence of my heart's desire and produce it every Christmas. When I was little, he bought me every kind of baby doll sold at that time. To my delight, most of them wet and cried and called me 'Mama'. When I was two, he found a three-foot-tall walking and talking doll with a record player inside her chest. To hear my mother tell it, he went back to the store twice - once to buy a recording to extend her vocabulary and once to get her a different outfit. The doll was bigger than I was and would have crushed me had she ever fallen over.

When I was in my Dale Evans period, Papa bought me a whole cowgirl outfit from a ten 'pint' hat to red boots to a stick pony named 'Susie'. Thrilled, I raced around our tiny house yelling 'Hi Ho Susie'. Okay, so I may have mixed up my cowpokes but it worked for me. In my Shirley Temple phase a couple years later, he gave me a leotard, shiny black tap shoes and a pink tutu. Delighted, I danced up and down our front stoop singing *The Good Ship Lollipop* at the top of my lungs - until the neighbors complained.

He and I shared a love of fantastical transportation too. Every year he bought himself a new automobile and me an evolving ride of some sort. At four, a tricycle sat under the tree. At five, there was a shiny blue 'Kidillac' pedal car. At six, he upgraded me to a bike. At eleven, he gave me a red go-cart that went twelve miles an hour.

As time went by, puberty rendered me awkward and chubby. No longer cute, I struggled to find myself in this new and strange body. Still, Papa gave me marvelous gifts focused on reinforcing my girlish dreams - a sterling silver charm bracelet, can-can petticoats trimmed in blue and pink ribbon, fancy salt and pepper sets for my collection. By the time I was thirteen, I no longer jumped on my presents with childish exuberance but sat on the couch pretending I was invisible while Christmas went on around me.

That was the year Papa dropped a large box in my lap and winked. Startled, I pulled the big blue ribbon off the package and ripped away the heavy white wrapping paper. It was from one of the fancy ladies' dress shops in our town. It was quiet in the room. I looked around. Everyone else was finished and watching me. This was the last unopened gift. I lifted off the lid and folded back the tissue paper. It was a Jackie Kennedy style white silk suit with a fur collar and jeweled buttons on the jacket. Dazed, I looked up.

"Go try it on." Papa smiled.

"Yesssss!" I clambered over the Christmas litter and dashed to my room. Standing in front of the mirror, I held the beautiful garment to my cheek and wondered if they'd let me have high heels and stockings to go with it. Maybe a brassiere. I closed my eyes imagining myself a woman instead of a gawky kid. Stripping off my pajamas, I slipped on the jacket. It was huge in the bust and tight around my midsection. I sucked in my stomach. The skirt flared over my non-existent hips and hung almost to my ankles.

"We'll take it back and get something more appropriate," my mother said when I came back into the living room. "Something that will fit."

"No. I love it." It was a whine.

"You can't breathe."

"We can let it out can't we?"

"Why did you buy that?" My dad frowned at Papa. "It's too grown up and it doesn't fit her."

Papa looked into my eyes. "But it will - and it won't be long now."

"Thank you, thank you, thank you." My hug nearly strangled him before I scurried back to my bedroom to look at myself in the mirror one more time.

My parents didn't let me keep the suit, of course. They returned it and bought 'kid clothes' the next week. Demoted back into ugly adolescence after a taste of adulthood, it was five years before I became the woman my grandfather envisioned. In fact, I wore a suit similar to the one he bought me when I got married - but Papa wasn't there for the ceremony. He died a few months after he gave me his last present - recognition of who I was and who I would be. No one has ever given me more.

I May Not Know Much

I may not know much, but I know what I want. Back in 2000, enough money to buy a new car landed in my hot little hand. I hurried to my computer and created a decision model complete with selection criteria and weighting factors. Okay, so I'm a little intense.

I wanted a car that would last forever. I typed in "Durable" and rated it a nine. I wasn't crazy about vans, trucks or SUVs. Tiny cars weren't my cup of tea either. I gave "Mid-Size" a weighting factor of seven. "Luxury" was a ten - non-negotiable. I love winding roads so "Stick" was an eight. I gave "Brand" a five. On second thought, I didn't give a damn about brand. I deleted the five and typed in a four point five. Getting lost is my special talent so "Navigation System" was also a ten. I scrolled up and down my list. Was that all I wanted? Oh yes, color. All cars are supposed to be red. I gave "Color" a nine.

On the Internet, I reviewed the major brands and added fifteen columns to my spreadsheet with the names of cars that caught my eye like "BMW", "Volvo" and "Saab". I included "Corvette" and "Mercedes" to be playful and "Wrangler" to be adventurous. I checked off the features that I wanted, multiplied them by the weighting factor and added up a final score for each model. Then I picked the top ten on the list. I was loaded for bear.

On the weekend, I began my search. My husband went with me "for laughs", he said.

The first place we stopped was the Volvo dealership. The salesman shook Johnny's hand. "I'm Bill."

"I'm John and this is my wife, Joyce."

Bill ignored me. "What can I do for you, John?"

"Not me - her."

I grinned and saluted.

Bill's smile melted. "Interested in a station wagon?"

"I want a mid-sized red sedan with a stick shift, navigation system and a luxury package."

"Well, now young lady, I don't keep that kind of thing on hand." He played with his glasses. "We sell to families, you understand. To women."

I raised an eyebrow.

"Women don't know how to drive standard transmissions," he explained.

"They don't?"

"I buy a stick and it'll sit here for months."

"But Volvo makes them." I persisted.

"Oh yeah, they make them, but I don't buy them. Same way with those nav systems."

"You could order one for me."

"It could take months to get something like that."

"I'll wait."

"It would cost more."

I gritted my teeth. "How much more?"

"We'd have to sit down and figure that out, now wouldn't we?"

Johnny snorted and busied himself with a rack of brochures.

"Why don't you take a look at this vehicle?" Bill opened the door of a dark blue station wagon. "I sell three or four a month to ladies in your age bracket."

I bit my tongue and peered inside. It was an automatic transmission but it did have leather seats. "How much?"

"If it's a little upscale for you, I can offer you a more basic model."

I focused on his carotid artery. "Does it come in red?"

"No one wants red."

Just as I sprang for the man's throat, Johnny grabbed my arm and ushered me out. "I think we've seen enough here."

🚗 🚗 🚗

Corvettes were our next stop. A bright shiny red one sat on a turntable in the middle of the showroom. It was a six speed too. The salesman shook Johnny's hand and pretended not to notice me. "So, John, want to take her out for a drive?"

"Not me - her!"

The young man turned to me. "Are you a librarian?"

"A what?" I glanced at Johnny. The corner of his mouth quivered.

"A librarian."

"No. Can we take it out?"

"It's a two seater."

51

"Yeah?" I wasn't sure what the problem was.

"Can you drive a six speed?"

"Like the wind."

The salesman looked over his shoulder at his boss, a heavy-set man with a goatee who shook his head.

"It was too expensive anyway." Johnny consoled me as we left the showroom.

"How do these guys sell anything?" I grumped. "I come to them knowing what I want - willing to wait until they get it, willing to pay cash. You'd think I'd be a preferred customer."

"They want to sell you something out of their inventory."

"I don't want what they have."

"They want to loan you the money too."

"So I'm a three time loser - special order, cash and a woman?"

"It's worse than that. They think you are a librarian." He slapped his leg and cackled.

🚙 🚙 🚙

"You don't really want a Wrangler do you?" Johnny said as we arrived at the Jeep dealership.

"No, but watch me take this one." I was in a cruel mood.

The Wrangler sat up on a pedestal. I crawled in and closed the door behind me.

A middle-aged man ran up to the car. "Can I help you?"

I put both hands on the steering wheel. "How would you flip one of these?"

52

"That was nasty," Johnny said at lunch. "And you wonder why salesmen are afraid of you."

"They aren't afraid of me. They are mean to me."

"They don't treat you any different than they do other women."

"Is that supposed to comfort me?" I bit into my sandwich and made a face.

"It is bizarre. Honda and Toyota will give you a standard transmission, but not with the luxury package. You can't even order it from the factory." He shook his head.

"Maybe there's a study somewhere that says people who drive a stick are allergic to leather." Frustration made me sarcastic.

"The dealership will install a nav system though."

"I want it to come from the factory."

"You are too picky."

"I know what I want."

The waitress freshen our drinks. "Is everything okay?"

"You know, I'd rather have mustard than mayonnaise on this." I handed her my plate.

"It comes with mayonnaise." She handed it back.

I sighed.

It was late afternoon when we pulled into the Acura dealership. The day had been a bust. Saab didn't have red.

Mercedes didn't have a stick. BMW was too expensive. I had a stomachache - probably because I ate that damned sandwich with mayonnaise.

"Hellooo." A freckled-faced woman hailed us as we parked. "Make yourself at home, I'll be right there."

"At least she acknowledged me as a customer." I muttered out of the side of my mouth.

"Don't be bitter." Johnny cautioned.

"So what did you have in mind?" The woman wore a pin identifying her as 'Marcie'.

"I want a mid-sized sedan, leather seats, electric windows, red with a navigation system and a stick shift."

"I can do everything but the standard - and you might have to wait for the color. I got a sports shifter though."

"What the hell is a sports shifter?"

"A fake stick." Marcie elbowed me. "For folks who can't drive a real one."

I dropped my head, defeated. "Show me the car."

Johnny chuckled as I followed Marcie into the display room.

It's Not About What You've Lost

It was a large area filled with treadmills and exercise equipment. Like all gyms, a dozen or more beautiful people lifted weights, did abdominal crunches and stretched out sore muscles. Most wore sweatshirts, shorts and tennis shoes. Some worked with a trainer. Others went through carefully choreographed routines designed to maximize their physical prowess. Each focused inward - intent on achieving some personal goal. The only difference between this room and thousands of others scattered across the country was that these young men and women were wounded Marines and soldiers, newly returned from Iraq and Afghanistan.

I stood in the doorway gripping a canvas bag filled with books and journals.

"Excuse me." The voice behind me was respectful.

I turned. A tall boy sitting in a wheel chair waited for me to move out of his way. One leg was missing just below the knee. The other was propped out in front of him - splinted and skewered and pinned together. His foot was bare - the toes black and yellow.

"Oh, I'm sorry." I moved out of the way - sorry for many things. He smiled as the nurse pushed him into the room.

My friend, Eddie Beesley - a Vietnam veteran who is a double amputee, rolled up to the young Marine and shook his hand. Connie, Eddie's wife, chattered like a canary. Her bubbly presence filled the room with light. The two of them worked together - encouraging, inspiring. I admired them. They were already touching hearts.

I was frozen - my eyes still locked on the horrendous wounds. A pretty black woman sat on a large cushion. Her skin glowed in the florescent lighting. Her left thigh ended in an elasticized sleeve. Her right leg was smooth and well-toned, just like her left one had been a few weeks ago. A boy in an electric wheel chair zoomed past. He was missing both legs, an arm and three fingers of his remaining hand.

I shook off my shyness and began to hand out journals - encouraging each person to use it to write down his thoughts for his children. Some reached for them eagerly. One young soldier said he wished he'd had one sooner. Another thanked me and tucked it into a large pocket in his backpack. I watched him walk away on his new legs. A few feet away, he paused to flirt with a cute girl who'd just come into the room.

A beefy Marine wanted the journal to keep track of his 'reps'. He was a weight-lifter before he'd been hurt. It was different now, but he was still a weight-lifter. He flexed a massive bicep to show me.

An older amputee sat beside his wife - massaging his stump. She held his brand new prosthesis. I handed him a journal. Connie introduced herself - and launched into all the ways she and Eddie had dealt with disability. With just a few words, she made everyone realize that as awful as these wounds are, these young people are still vital, still sexy, still powerful - still alive.

As we left, the soldier in the electric wheelchair zipped past us again. This time, I didn't see his afflictions - but the mischievous sparkle of an eighteen-year-old boy. We waved at him as the elevator doors closed.

Beware a Dark Horse!

Isn't a mare a female horse?" I asked my dad when I was eight.

"Yep." He hid behind his morning newspaper. He did that when he didn't want me to bother him with questions.

"It doesn't make any sense then."

"What doesn't?"

"Nightmares."

"You've been having nightmares?"

"No. I've just been wondering about them."

He lowered his newspaper. "What do you mean?"

"Maybe they are dark horses."

"What?"

"Nightmares." I sighed in exasperation.

"Nightmares are bad dreams," he said.

"But why do they call them nightmares?"

"I don't know."

"Maybe they are more than that. Maybe they are real. Maybe they gallop through your room at night and since you are too sleepy to wake up, it scares you and when you do wake up you can't figure out what happened and so you think you've had a bad dream."

"Eat your breakfast, Joyce."

Of Grandmas and Cowboys

I'm a big believer in following the rules of the road. I obey traffic lights and signs. I stay back from the vehicle ahead of me by one car length for every ten miles an hour I'm traveling. I observe speed limits. I signal when turning or changing lanes. I try to be courteous - letting people merge in front of me, using my brake lights to warn folks behind me of changing traffic conditions, beeping my horn only to warn of danger. I try not to make any blunders although as a human being, I inevitably do - and when others make mistakes, I try to be understanding. Pardon me while I adjust my halo.

Most of the folks I share the road with seem to be as angelic as I am. We drive sedate white sedans and station wagons. Our smiles are dazzling and our wings are only for show. Of course, there are a few hellions out there - usually driving shiny red sports cars, who believe the road was built for their private use. They resent any other vehicles that deign get in their way. Then there are demons. They believe it is their mission in life to teach the rest of us a lesson. For some reason, they usually drive dirty black SUVs.

The guys in the sports cars - it's almost always a guy - drive like the wind. If an angel like me happens to be cruising along in the fast lane less than twenty miles an hour above the speed limit, the hellion will beep his horn and flash his lights. Then before you can move out of his way, he swerves to the right, passes and then slips back in front of you to disappear at warp speed into the gloaming. He never brakes at all if he can avoid it. If you are in the white sedan, it feels like those old cartoons where the hare rushes by so fast that the tortoise is left spinning around on his shell.

The ladies in the dirty SUVs - it's almost always a woman - don't feel that it's enough that they pass you. They want to make you as unhappy as your mere existence has made them - sort of a tit-for-tat technique. Demons lay on the horn for several minutes - long blasts designed to scare an innocent angel out of his or her argyles - and then as the seconds tick by, to set the heart a pumping and the nerves a grating. You signal and try to merge to your right. The irate fem follows you - her front bumper inches from your rear end. If traffic clears, she might zoom around you - glaring and cursing. Then, if a demon feels you haven't been punished enough, she'll cut in front of you and hit her brakes. As you fight to control your station wagon, she'll accelerate with one slim arm stuck out her driver's side window, a delicate manicured middle finger extended in the air.

Most angels need to pull off the highway for ice cream at that point. That's why you see so many white cars at Dairy Queens.

Other characters on the road in lesser numbers are the cowboys and the grandmas. Cowboys drive great big pickup trucks, of course. Lots of times they have duel back wheels with knobby mud tires that have never ever seen mud. You can get along fine with cowboys as long as you don't splash road grit on their high gloss side panels. They respond with delight to compliments about the 'Lil Squirt' decals on the back window. Of course, these are the guys with gun racks and guns. If you are a demon driving a dirty black SUV, try not to tick them off.

Grandmas drive old cars that look like brand new - and they drive them really slow. Faded yellow Cadillacs and Lincolns are the norm but occasionally you'll see them driving a twenty-year-old Buick or Oldsmobile. They brake for leaves blowing across the street and signal a half mile before making their turn. They stay off freeways and highways because everyone drives too fast. There's too much traffic on boulevards and avenues - and back roads are too winding or hilly or dark or lonely for them. Afraid of rain, snow and ice, you see them on bright sunny days on the way to the doctor, the hairdresser or Wal-Mart. The thing about grandmas is that even though they annoy everyone, no one is nasty to them - not even demons. Hellions give them wide berth. Angels nod and smile as they pass. You see cowboys stopping to help grandmas find medical clinics, which seem to have moved since their last visit a month ago.

Survival on America's highways depends on strategic avoidance of hazards, keeping a cool head and luck. Maintaining your current speed and position is best when set upon by a high-spirited hellion bent on reaching the horizon. They view the road as an obstacle course through which they must maneuver. You are just another obstacle. When faced with a raving demon, concentrate on whether you will get an M&M Blizzard or a chocolate dip. Getting angry won't help the situation. Eventually someone else will frustrate her more than you and you will be free to join your colleagues at the Dairy Queen.

Stay clear of cowboys on days when there is ice on the streets. They are likely to spin around in front of you with no warning - gripping their steering wheels with white knuckles - eyes and mouths wide. However, they are a minor threat. Even if they do have a snow blade for the front of the pickup, they are apt to keep the truck inside an environmentally controlled garage on bad days.

Don't worry about grandmas. They aren't going where you are going anyway.

Roll the Dice and Cross Your Fingers

Did you ever ponder the basic idea of insurance? I'm sure it was devised by some half-crazed imp drunk on blue soda pop with a twisted sense of humor. As best I can figure, insurance is a gamble where you bet against yourself. You wager you are going to have an accident, the insurance company asserts that you won't. If you DO have an accident, you win and they lose. How weird is that?

When you think about all the different kinds of insurance, it gets even stranger. There's flood insurance where you posit that a great wave is going to come wash your house away. The insurance company takes your money because they think the rains won't come any time soon - especially since you live on a hill and there's no river, lake or pond anywhere near you. You think you're gonna get sick but the HMO is sure that you won't - and if you do, they are going to turn down your claim anyway. Metlife is glad to take your money when you are worried about having a toothache sometime in the future. Paranoid people can protect against robbery, broken glass and fire. Farmers can cover their crops for a price. There's malpractice insurance for doctors, lawyers and engineers. I presume you buy those and other liability policies thinking you're gonna screw up.

Some companies cater to folks with serious phobias - like fear of catastrophic sickness or dismemberment. (These same people watch Lifetime movies and all the Freddie Kruger flicks.) You can insure body parts, relatives, friends and possessions. You can protect your wages, your savings, your pets, your basement and your ideas. That must be in case ideas cause someone harm - sort of the anti-evil eye thing. Of course, a witch doctor could perform the same function for a single fee instead of an endless stream of premiums, but that's fodder for a different shriek. The funniest is life insurance, where you only get paid if you die - and you can't enjoy it anyway because someone else collects. Who thought of that one?

When I worked for the Gas Company, someone came up with the great idea of weather insurance. I couldn't bend my mind around that one. Were we betting that there would or wouldn't be weather?

Some people buy insurance for the **investment**. Now I ask you, why would I do that when I have credit card companies begging me to transfer my balances to them? The good news is that my credit cards are protected in case someone steals them and buys a Porsche. What I don't understand is who pays for that insurance? I'm sure it's me - I just can't figure out how.

Then there are the extended warranties. You buy them to protect yourself after your manufacturer's guarantee on some big-ticket item expires. They sell them for just about everything now – from electronics to beds to organs -the kind you play, not the kind in and on your body. These days, cashiers ask if you want to gamble that your iPod will die an early death or that your laptop screen will supernova ninety-one days after purchase. I can understand spending a few extra bucks in case my new television explodes, but the other day the salesperson asked me if I wanted to buy an extended warranty on a hundred and fifty dollar digital voice recorder the size of a fat pencil. Get real. I'll lose that sucker long before it breaks.

There are plenty of companies betting that earthquakes won't happen in Florida, and hurricanes won't make it to Minneapolis. I get that part. What I don't get is - are there any Minneapolitans out there willing to put money on the possibility of a hurricane? It gets even more confusing when you start talking pork belly futures and collars and floors. My dad used to say there's a sucker born every minute - and he was probably right. The thing of it is, I'm pretty sure he was taking about me.

Is there anyone out there willing to bet me that I'll get back the money I lost on Enron stock?

Right.

I didn't think so.

Don't Let the Big Bugs Byte?

Folks who man help desks deal with a lot of stupid questions. I can sympathize with that. In fact, having worked in and with I/T for years, I have a bag full of stories that are funny because they are outstandingly stupid. You know the ones I mean. "My computer says it doesn't recognize my printer even after I held it up in front of the monitor and introduced them", "I don't *have* an 'any' key" and "I can't *find* the sloppy disk" make me laugh harder than Richard Pryor and George Carlin put together - even now.

It started back years ago when the whole concept of personal computing was new. The look of wide-eyed horror on my secretary's face when I contacted another computer with my new modem and it answered me back in English was priceless. Okay, I'll admit I set her up. It's something that the wicked do to the innocent. I'll probably fry in hell for it, but it sure was fun when my buddy on the other computer accurately described what the sweet lady was wearing. At least, I waited until I got to the bathroom where I cackled all alone in my stall.

It's a game, you see.

When someone loses their mind while using a computer, those of us they ask for help enjoy the moment so much that we seek to make the mirth last by doing a little chain yanking. For example, one time I walked by and noticed my boss staring at a blank screen with a "C" prompt in the bottom left corner. I offered to help him but he said, "That's okay. It'll boot up here in a minute." At that point, the devil made me go back to my desk and pretend to work until he gave up waiting a half hour later and asked me how I made the damned thing work. "Magic," I said with my sunniest smile. He frowned and scratched his head. "Is that case sensitive?" I didn't quite make it to the bathroom that time.

The paranoia engendered by this chain yanking, mixed with real concerns like viruses and worms, has left the innocent worried about how to protect themselves from alien invaders. One fellow told me that he turned off his computer every night to prevent hackers from stealing his novel. "What makes you think anyone is trying to steal your work?" I asked. "Because whenever I leave the computer on, there are errors in my manuscript the next morning." "I see." I smothered my bemusement. "So you think Internet gremlins are accessing your hard drive and putting mistakes in your book?" He stiffened at my sarcasm. "Well, it sure the hell isn't me."

"Right."

Of course, I've had my share of computer mishaps which are never as funny as when the joke is on the other guy. Back in the olden days when there were no hard drives, programs ran off a system disk in your left floppy drive and worked on the data you kept in a second floppy disk on the right. Never one to conclusively identify left and right, I got them mixed up. Not to worry, a message appeared at my c prompt. "Do you really want to delete the System Disk?" I was outraged at the condescending question. "Hell, yes," I muttered and hit the "Yes" option. "NOOOO," I howled when I recognized my mistake but it was too late to call it back. While trying to explain this lapse in judgment to the guys in I/T, I fell backwards into a large box of paper that fit exactly onto my derrière. It had to be pulled off by overly polite, red-faced techs who I *knew* were gonna laugh as soon as the automatic door closed behind me - but that's another story.

So you see, I understand the temptation. I'm sure that dealing with the inanity of the general public hour after hour, day in and day out, gets old even to the most patient techie. However, these guys are getting younger every year - and sillier. Who do they think they are talking to? Some yo-yo who doesn't know a Ram from a Rom? Who do they think *designed* all these systems that they know so much about?

Okay, so I didn't design the Internet or home computers or any of the cool games - but people of my generation did, for crying out loud.

The other day I had to call Hajeeb Telecommie about my new laptop that had just come back from the repair shop. I guess Hajeeb and I just got off on the wrong foot. Maybe I was a little tense. Perhaps he'd had a long day. Who knows why Hajeeb decided to play me. Knowing what he was doing was no defense, and he won the day and is probably cackling in his own bathroom this very moment.

"Turn over your laptop," he told me. "We are going to reset the infarculator."

"Okay." I heard snickering in the background and adjusted the volume on my Bluetooth headset.

"See the indentation?"

The bottom of the computer was flat as a pancake. "No."

"See the protrusion?" His voice trembled as he choked on his own joke.

"No."

"It's below the indentation."

"You mean the battery?"

"You can call it that." More snickering.

"What do you want me to do with it?"

"Take it out."

"Okay."

"Is it out?"

"Yes."

"Put it back in."

I gritted my teeth. "Okay."

"Now, let's reinstall the program."

"Okay." I turned the laptop right side up and gazed into the monitor.

"See where it says "Click here"?"

"Yes."

"Don't."

"Don't click?"

"Don't click there."

"Where should I click?"

"See the blue button?"

"Yes."

"There."

"Okay." I clicked.

A sudden gasp made me jump. "Did you click?" He sounded desperate.

"Yeah."

"Good."

Now I know why people write viruses - to get back at nerds like Hajeeb.

Remember When I Said . . .

He was on the make when he said it. "I've been in love with you for over a year." The words made me smile. It was our first date back in 1967. Did he really think I was going to buy that one? I turned to look at him expecting a leer, but he seemed dead serious. Could it be? Then I saw the twinkle in his eye and the sly half smile on his lips. Naw!

When we were married a few months later on a Thursday afternoon after bowling, we spent our wedding night camped out on the banks of Beaver Lake. I snuggled up next to him and whispered in his ear. "Remember our first date when you said you'd been in love with me for a year?"

"Uh huh." He stared into the campfire.

"Was it true?" I stroked his face, expecting to stoke the fires of my ego with his answer.

"Hell, no." He laughed and pinched my cheek. "But it was a great line, don't you think?"

Over the years, I've learned to deal with this man whose greatest pleasure in life is to drive me crazy. Like the time he convinced me to climb a tree with him and then left me dangling out on the limb while he tickled me and took photos. Or the time he mooned me during an argument when I paused to answer a long distance phone call from my mother. Or the time he hid the last puzzle piece - for days. There was the jumping out from behind the door naked caper and the glass of ice water tossed over the shower door incident. To top that while we were vacationing in Kenya and lions were prowling outside our cabin, he grabbed my toe in the middle of the night and growled.

Before we realized the impossibility of sharing a personal computer, he spent each evening rearranging the Windows desktop. I spent every morning for weeks, shaking my head and tsk, tsk, tsking - trying to figure out why my configuration wasn't being saved. Then one day, I caught him peeking around the door jamb at me and chuckling. It was a repeat exercise from the great rear view mirror war of the mid 1970s and an early skirmish over the best way to fold towels in the late 1960s.

Once we went to the movies to see *Fiddler on the Roof* but the line was too long and we ended up watching *JAWS*. On the way home, I vowed never to set foot in the ocean again - especially not alone in the moonlight and especially not naked. In fact, in my vehemence, I threatened to boycott the bathtub. That night I dreamed my husband sat up in bed, lifted my nightgown and bit me on the belly. I squealed and jumped up to find him snoring beside me, peacefully drooling into his pillow. Feeling like a fool, I punched my own pillow a few times before sinking back into an uneasy sleep filled with protruding fins and serrated teeth. A decade later at a cocktail party, I told the story of how the movie had so unnerved me that I had this weird nightmare. While my audience tittered, I caught that smug little smirk he used to indicate a 'gotcha'.

A year past our thirtieth wedding anniversary, I sat up in bed watching a movie while he catnapped beside me. As the heroine ran shrieking from the haunted house in the driving rain, he opened his eyes. "Hey," he whispered drowsily.

"What?" The woman teetered at the edge of the cliff as the wind whipped her hair and skirt.

"Remember back when we first got married?"

I kept my eyes on the flickering TV screen. "Yeah."

"Remember when I told you I lied about loving you for a year before we started dating?"

The earth crumbled beneath the heroine's feet and she grabbed the root of a tree as she fell. "Yeah?"

"I lied."

I turned to look at him, but he was pretending to be asleep.

DNA

I have my father's eyes - even though his were dark brown and mine are light green. I think that is why I never saw things quite the same way that he did. We were imperfect doppelgangers - he glittered and I admired the shine. He struggled and I appreciated the effort. He suffered for friends lost long before I was born - I spent a childhood hearing about them and a lifetime writing about them as if they were **my** friends.

I have my mother's laugh. I hear her in my phone mail greeting - and that first moment when I speak into a microphone. I feel her with me when I'm happy - and that makes me wonder if whispers and dreams are also the stuff of DNA.

My Nanny Frankie donated her hair to my gene pool - and her sense of adventure. I have a picture of her decked out in a long-waisted, short-skirted flapper outfit. It makes me smile whenever I see it - and remember how we preened together in front of the mirror when I was a curly-headed urchin and she a forty-year old grandmother.

My Nanny Viola gave me her high cheekbones and her distinctive nose. She gave them to my Aunt Mary too - they are especially beautiful on her. Those features are the only part of our Cherokee heritage that remains - and I passed them on to my daughter and son.

I have my Papa Bud's ivory white skin that burns under a sixty-Watt light bulb. He and I spent hours under the shade tree in his back yard while everyone else ran around outside - oblivious to that evil yellow ball in the sky. He made me feel less alone in my vulnerability.

I have my Great Aunt Frances' lips. They were a lovely complement to her copper-colored eyes and creamy skin. On me, they seem rather unremarkable - although I play them up just like she did. I also share one of her flaws. She was unremittingly blunt - often mistaking opinion for honesty. When I speak sharply, I think of her and bite my tongue - hoping to call back my thoughtless words - lest I wound the tender souls around me like she wounded me.

At five foot seven, my Uncle Jimmy was the tallest of my father's family - and if you look in the dictionary under the word "loyal," you will see his picture. I was never as tall as Uncle Jimmy - but I aspire to be.

I loved my Aunt Pete. She had a wry twinkle in her smile. When I was a kid, I'd borrow her tangerine lipstick and stretch my newly-oranged mouth in a twisted imitation of her dazzle - that was before I realized that inner glow can't be copied.

I called my Papa Paul's second wife Gingie. She is my third grandmother in every sense of the word. She combined beauty, grace and creativity into one package. Can DNA be transferred by osmosis – or love?

My great grandpa George, crippled by wood alcohol when he was nineteen, wove slings to hoist himself up onto the houses that he built - to nail down shingles and paint shutters. I pray for his determination whenever I feel overwhelmed.

My second cousin Hugh is a kind and gentle intellectual. He and my mother were close friends. Whenever something nice happens to me, he is one of the first people I want to tell - because it is almost like telling my Mama that I did good. Did I inherit his passion for literature - and achievement - or hers?

Then there's my Papa Paul – murdered when I was thirteen. He was strong, passionate, stubborn and intense. It wasn't until I was in my fifties that I realized that he paid for my dancing lessons - and my private school tuition - the beautiful clothes that I wore and the cool toys I owned. I went to college because the life insurance policy he took out on himself when I was born was double indemnity. I owe him so much and hope that some part of him lives on in me.

I like to think that I'm an old soul come to fruition at this place and time by design - but maybe I'm a DNA stew and the weaknesses of my ancestors will trip me up too. Still, each time I gaze into the mirror, I see multitudes staring back - and I'm grateful.

Ode to the Odd

We are a diverse species. However, most of us prefer to live in groups that share common characteristics. It's comforting to hang out with folks who mirror our looks and predilections. Homogeneity just feels good. We enjoy people who share our dreams, schemes and nose shapes. It feels safe and familiar. Oh, we accept minor deviations. Dolly Parton's natural attributes are outside the norm but she is viewed with awed appreciation. However, we have to force ourselves to make room for those who are inherently different. The unusually tall or small must deal with a world that doesn't fit. Handicapped folks face barriers that most of us never consider. It takes effort to shuffle the cards and sort ourselves based on things that matter rather than unimportant externalities.

However, sometimes the things that separate us from the crowd are not obvious at first glance. We call those characteristics "eccentricities". Everyone is odd in some way. My son, Nate, taps his heel - constantly. My husband has a grudge against the bank - any bank, all banks. My cousin Karen loves her things to be purple - clothes, cars, keys, toasters, computers, cell phones, etc. In my travels, I met a man who blinked twice, lifted his hat and replaced it on his head every five minutes. I knew a girl in college who kept knitting needles under her pillow - just in case. She could never adequately explain the circumstance that would necessitate their retrieval. An emergency knitting project, maybe?

In my case, I have two eccentricities. First, I am geographically challenged. It's not that I don't know where I'm going, it's just that I don't know where I am now. Apparently, my ancestors were neither gatherers nor hunters so I was born without the orientation gene. Second, I can't open anything. From aspirin bottles to shrink-wrapped items from Amazon, packaged goods deny me their contents with frustrating regularity. Doors, locks, purses and file cabinets give me trouble too - as do websites, ATM machines and brassiere clasps. I have an equally contentious relationship with electronic products sealed inside molded plastic. I can see the object of my desire but neither teeth nor scissors nor blow torches can pry it loose.

You might say that these two peculiarities aren't all that bad. Weird, yes - but small in the overall scheme of things. True, it's not like Jack Nicholson's character in "As Good as it Gets" who needed to turn the lights on, off, on, off and on each time he entered a room. It's not nearly as strange as my friend Mindy who's afraid of wind or my friend Dale who's afraid of weather or my friend Peter who rates dirt. However, my personal brand of craziness does have its drawbacks.

For example, the other day I was reading up on self-defense techniques. Given my two failings, it was a frightening list of tips:

- **If you sense problems on your way, just change your route.** Change my route? Are you kidding? I get lost on the way to the bathroom. No way am I going to risk being attacked when I don't know where I am - which is most of the time.

- **Do not wear conspicuous jewelry when you are walking the streets alone.** What good is jewelry if it's not conspicuous? Especially after it took me thirty minutes to get it out of the box and around my neck.

- **Do not act or look like an easy target.** Okay, what does an easy target look like? Someone told me that my long hair gives a bad guy something to grab. Seems to me if he was going to grab something, he'd go for the conspicuous jewelry.

- **Don't hitchhike.** Well, duh.

- **Don't pull over to the side of a dark, lonely road even if a stranger gestures for you to.** Double duh.

- **Don't get in a taxi that has a central locking mechanism.** Now this is down right terrifying for a person who can't open a mustard jar. How many taxis don't have a central locking mechanism these days? Now I have nightmares about trying to unlock a locked taxi on a dark, lonely road. Sometimes the stranger is waiting for me to get out, sometimes he's in the taxi with me. EEEK!

- **Go for your attackers gonads.** Get real. I want to stay as far away from them as possible - and besides, I have trouble with zippers too.

By the way, does anyone want to take a shot at unlocking my medic alert bracelet?

Sexiness and the Wizard

L et's talk about sex – or more precisely, sexiness. It's an intriguing topic. There are few conversations men love more. Stop any gum-popping dude on the corner and they will rhapsodize about the qualities sexy women share – large eyes, small noses, big lips, slim but round bodies, soft skin. Oh there are variations on their passions. Large breasts may excite a stray cowboy here or there. Long legs might move a businessman or a basketball player. A shrink might go for a plump butt, a circus clown for big feet. A guy I've known since we were in college once told me that he was a "systems' man." "It's the whole package," he said. "If the thighs are too pudgy but the smile is bright, the lady passes muster. If the hair is too curly but she's fun to be around, then she's okay by me." Larry is, of course, an engineer.

We women have our own list of preferences - and no, guys, the one thing you worry about isn't an issue for most of us. Oh sure, when we are young, it's the DNA thing, whether we know it or not. Who doesn't want the smartest, healthiest, most beautiful children? Darwin probably got the idea for his theory when he was in high school, watching the jocks pair off with the homecoming princesses. At that age, muscles and hairy chests are cool. Square jaws, cleft chins and broad shoulders are popular. Being able to spit sunflower seeds across the biology room is an important skill. Then we grow up. Running and jumping and bouncing a ball impressed me for about a minute and a half when I was thirteen. Then other things took over.

Conventionally sexy people appear on the covers of magazines and in movies. Most of them are babies. Oh sure, once in a while someone beautiful like Clint Eastwood turns up - and once in a while, someone like George Clooney graduates in my mind from silly dork to hot dude. Men seem more comfortable with labeling people whose facial bone structure hasn't yet firmed up as "interesting" which is, of course, a euphemism.

The mothering thing has destroyed a lot of art for me. Michelangelo's David, while gorgeous, makes me want to buy him a pair of Vans, loud swim trunks and a surfboard. Jake Gyllenhaal will always be a rocket kid - I can't deal with him as a gay cowboy. He's the latest in a long line of young actors that suddenly grew up. Macaulay Culkin would still be home alone if it were up to me. Heck, I've convinced myself that Cubbie O'Brien still wears Mouseketeer ears - and he's older than me. The movie Phantom didn't do it for me like some of his stage counterparts. It's not that Gerard Butler wasn't good. It's that I felt the urge to cut his meat and encourage him to eat his peas.

For my money, smart, funny and sunny equals sexy. Grumps are boring - who wants to hang out with someone whose emails are written in all caps? I like scintillating conversation - you know the kind where the *real* topic is sex but everyone else thinks you are discussing dessert? Show-offs are okay if they have something to show - and I don't mean body parts. I'm not nuts about men who think honesty is a synonym for meanness. If I'm not perfect, have a heart and tell me that I am.

Seems to me that sexy and beautiful are two different things. Sure, some folks are blessed with both accolades by their admirers, but most of us would be tickled to be called one or the other. Then there are those poor souls who can't honestly be called either. That's why convincing insincerity is such an important skill - "Yes, Louise, you look lovely in that - er, delightful shade of puce" - or, "Norm, you've grown a new you." That's why soap, cosmetics and drugs are so close to each other in the Wal-Mart. After you remove your warts, pluck the hairs out of your ears and wash away the dandruff, you can work on your repartee while buying Trojans.

Now if you can only find some kind-hearted liar out there.

Google, Googol and Love

Some marriages are held together by melodrama, others by children or shared beliefs. Comfort is the super glue for most. My long relationship is rooted in convoluted conversations over dinner.

"What do you call ten to the power of one hundred?" My husband Johnny asked the other night at Scoglio's.

"A really big number?"

"A googol." He loves to stump me.

"Google? Like the search engine?" I'm under-equipped to play guessing games with a man who uses his computer to search for prime numbers in his spare time - but I try.

"A googol was around a lot longer than Google," he pontificated.

I was sure there was a point coming, but I've been down this road many times in our years together. I decided to parry his thrust. "How much longer ?"

"Back in the 1930s."

"Okay." I would much prefer your basic knock-knock joke. At least I had a chance with them. If a googol was defined long before I was born, I'm obviously an idiot for not being familiar with the term.

"So what do you call ten to the power of a googol?"

"Googolocity?" It was a wild guess.

"Nope." The man can smell desperation a mile away

I wanted to go for his throat. "Googolicious?"

"Nope."

"Googolino?"

"You are getting colder."

I searched for a name for a number many orders of magnitude bigger than any I'd ever contemplated before. "What's wrong with infinity? That worked for Ben Casey."

"You're pouting," he said.

"No, I'm not."

"Yes, you are. Besides, that wasn't Ben Casey. That was Dr. Zorba."

"Yeah, Dr. Zorba. That's the guy." I'd been planning to counter his googol with a "lemniscate," but if he remembered Dr. Zorba, he probably knew what the infinity sign was called too.

"Well?"

I was out of ammunition. No other obscure word came to mind. "I give up. What do you call ten to the power of googol?"

"A googolplex."

I was speechless.

He raised an eyebrow.

"Wow." I offered and waited a moment before attacking. "Do you suppose Google chose that name for their search engine because they wanted to get a googol's worth of websites included in their index?"

84

"Could be," he said. "A few years ago when Google Whacking was popular they had a couple billion websites. Think how many they'll have in ten years? In thirty?"

Only my husband and the other lords of geek-dom could find nirvana by playing such a game. (Google Whackers put in a two-word query, and if Google found only one page with that combination, it was considered a 'whack'. Try it. It's harder than it sounds - and getting harder every day.) Anyway, I was relieved to get past the quiz part of the conversation and into the pondering part. "It'll get to the point where you can find everyone and everything on Google," I said.

"We're close," he agreed. "You can google just about anyone now."

"If I can't find myself on Google, I won't exist?"

"Maybe that's why they haven't found Osama bin Laden."

"What?"

"He's hiding out on Google and no one's thought to look for him there."

"Right." I rolled my eyes before I realized he might have something. "Maybe they should look for Jimmy Hoffa on Google."

"And the Holy Grail?" He smiled at me.

"Not the Holy Grail," I countered. "They found that in the *Da Vinci Code*."

We laughed together.

"Why exactly did you ask me about googols to begin with?" I asked.

He finished his dinner and wiped his lips with a napkin. "Because I love you a googol."

"What? Not a googolplex?"

It's worth waiting until the end of a nonsensical conversation if there's a googol's worth of love on the far side.

The Call of the Hare

E very once in a while, I wake up with a thought that just won't go away. About fifteen years ago, I had a dream about getting run over by a glacier. It was one of those cartoonie things where the slow-moving icy monolith squished me flat as the proverbial pancake. When I awoke, I knew that I was supposed to go to Alaska. I went to the office and did a little research on a cruise to our most northern state. Just before pulling the trigger on the pricey plan, it occurred to me that perhaps I should ask my husband if he had a problem with it.

His secretary answered the phone. "Hi Joyce," she said. "How are you?"

"I have a wild hair. Have Johnny call me before I spend a lot of money."

"Sure." She was a nice lady who shielded her charges like a bulldog guarding frankfurters. "I'll get him the message right away."

A few minutes later, she called back to set up a lunch date so Johnny and I could discuss my problem. Problem? That afternoon, over our chicken salads, I laid out my plans for an Alaskan vacation two months hence.

"Is **that** what this is about?" He asked.

"What else?"

"Something about a rabbit?"

"A rabbit?"

87

Snickering, Johnny pulled out the note his secretary had given him. "Call Joyce before she spends money on a wild hare."

Okay, I can understand the confusion. Not many people know about wild hairs. Most folks seem more rooted than me - more cautious in their approach to life. However, I do a lot of things simply because I can't bear **not** doing them - because I wake up with the thought lodged irritatingly in my brain like an infected pimple. Of course, not all of these impulsive decisions work out. The pair of pointy-toed cowboy boots that set in the back of my closet rub blisters on the backs of my calves. I didn't consider that possibility before plunking down my two hundred, twenty-five dollars.

Some of my ideas have short-term benefits that become long-term hassles. The Fiat Spider falls into that category. A convertible sports car in Florida is one thing, it's quite another in rainy, snowy Pittsburgh. The electric juicer was another ill-conceived purchase given that I don't like juice of any kind. Since no colorful dreams precipitated those unfortunate expenditures, I maintain that they were the result of nefarious marketing ploys that work only too well on the likes of me. I have to be ever wary of that when the urge to possess something too outlandish overwhelms me.

One time, the Almighty rescued me from a reckless act right in the middle of Sam's Club. I found a huge popcorn machine on wheels. I imagined it in our basement next to our home theater. I could hear the loud snaps as the kernels exploded into fluffy lil nuggets. In my mind's nose, I smelled it. Ah!

I was wrestling the huge contraption to the check out stand when God spoke to me. "Joyce," He said.

I looked around. There was no one else in the aisle but an old lady with a cart full of frozen waffles. "What?"

"If you buy that, you will have to clean it."

It was a good point. Have you ever noticed that most of God's suggestions turn out to be first-rate? I took the popcorn cart back and bought a box of Orville Redenbacher's. Every time we watch a movie while nibbling on a bowl of freshly popped corn, I thank God that there's no greasy machine waiting for me.

Then there was the time that I dreamed I was standing on a fence post with a Doberman Pincer leaping up to nip at my heels. I stretched out my arms and glided across his pen to safety on the other side. I awoke knowing that I had to learn to fly - that very day.

"Why do you think that means you have to learn to fly?" My husband asked. "Why doesn't it mean that you are supposed to buy a dog?"

I shook my head and rolled my eyes. "Because if I was supposed to buy a dog, the Doberman would have eaten me alive."

"Oh," he said.

Bubbles

I love bubbles. The word itself makes me smile. All those B's burbling through my lips like a babbling brook makes me think of a party. I remember going to a restaurant with a Hawaiian floor show years ago. After singing Don Ho tunes and swigging champagne for about an hour, dozens of tipsy ladies in flowered muumuus scurried for the restroom. The line snaked out the door and down the hall. By the time I got there, those of us left were in a silly mood. All the stalls were full. Women stood two deep at the sinks. The sound of running water filled our ears. Someone started singing, "Tiny bubbles." Pretty soon everyone joined in - some in harmony. Those who weren't singing were giggling and twirling their leis like hoola-hoops. It was pretty cool - all those strangers singing together. Okay, so it kinda flipped out our husbands when we trooped back to our tables humming. Hmm. Maybe you had to be there.

Back to bubbles. Ever watch children dance around when you bring out a bowl of soapy water and those weird little loop dealies? All those ephemeral spheres, glistening in the sunlight - and then, they pop! Just like that. How cool. They are refreshing and well - fun. You can just feel your blood pressure going down and the corners of your mouth going up when you encounter a bubble. At least, I can. Maybe that's why bubble wrap is so much fun. When I worked in that "other industry", my colleagues and I would gather in my office anytime anyone got anything new. We'd cut up the bubble wrap so that everyone got a piece. Then we'd sit around and discuss our problems while popping bubbles.

Some of us could get several to pop at once by squeezing it under our arms - a sort of BLOP! The best of us could get them to pop sequentially up and down the rows . . . pop, pop, pop, pop . . . like a bunch of firecrackers. It was noisy and oh, so soothing. Who needs a shrink when you've got bubble wrap? Okay, so maybe you had to be there for that one too.

Watching stuff boil is fun for that same reason. When I was a kid, the only way you got pudding was to mix the powdery contents of a Jello Pudding box with cold milk in a saucepan. My mom would put it on the stove and turn the burner on low. Then I'd stand on a stool and stir with a wooden spoon until it started getting thick. It was a little scary when it really got to going - sometimes the bubbles would pop and tiny bits of hot pudding would jump up and burn my hands. I'd squeal but keep on stirring with all the determination a five-year-old can muster. No way would a little burn keep me away from chocolate even then.

Of course, steaming cauldrons can be more problematic than that. You never know WHY they are bubbling. One time I bought a bottle of hot sauce and brought it home. It took me forever to open it. When I finally loosened the lid, it blew off and hit the ceiling. My husband came running to find my face and hair dripping with the sizzling red liquid. We cautiously peered into the wide-mouthed bottle. The sauce was alive. Bub bup, bub bup. All we needed was eye of newt and toe of lizard.

My husband turned to me. "Maybe we ought to get that off your face." As he dabbed the corrosive substance off the tip of my nose with a wet cloth, the sauce that was left in the bottle burbled louder.

"Let's go out to eat," I said.

"You got it." He nudged the bottle with a wooden spoon and it fell into the sink.

It was the last time I tried to cook anything. Okay, next to last - but that's another shriek.

It's interesting how time changes so many things - and yet some things remain constant. I just got a fancy Motorola Q phone. For a gizmo-loving person like me, it's nirvana. I can get my email on it. I can text message to my heart's delight. I have my calendar on it - and my task list. (You know, where you remind yourself of all the things you have to do? Things like, "Buy more hot sauce" or "Don't forget to transfer money from savings account to checking account before check to get Acura towed gets cashed.") I can use it to snap pictures of anyone likely to call me and then put it in my address book so that when they **do** call me, their pictures pop up. I can record their voices and store the file in my address book so that when they call me, they . . . well . . . **call** me. Think of the possible ring tones. "Hey, sweetheart. It's noon. Wake up" or "Get off the computer and answer your #$%^&* phone" or "Joyce, This is Warren Buffett calling. I have a present for you" or "Hey Mom. Got money?"

However, the coolest thing is that there is a game on my phone - and it's called "Bubble Breaker." No lie. It's a bunch of colored bubbles and the object of the game is to position the cursor over a bubble that has other bubbles of the same color touching it. When you click, it makes that multiple-bubble wrap popping sound in the Bluetooth ear piece. Way cool. I can feel my blood-pressure going down as we speak.

The other night, I was sitting in bed in the dark watching TV and playing Bubble Breaker on my phone.

My husband jerked awake when my Bluetooth ear piece flashed in the night.

"**What** are you doing?" he asked.

"Popping bubbles."

"Why?"

"It's relaxing."

"It's three am. Can't you sleep?"

"I'm going for a ten-pop string."

"Okay." He yawned and got up to go to the bathroom.

Just then my phone rang. "My record is fifteen pops at once. You can't beat that," it says. (Don't you just **love** those personalized ring tones?)

I answered. "You are calling me from the bathroom?"

"How did you know it was me?"

Tea and Empathy

Susan Sarandon is the divorced mother of two children. Julia Roberts is her ex-husband's new squeeze. At first, Susan resents Julia, but let's face it, who doesn't love Julia? Then we find out that Susan has some awful disease and that she's not going to make it. I sit in my recliner, my computer in my lap - fingers poised over the worn keyboard - unable to pull my eyes away from the television set.

The phone rings.

I snort back my grief for Susan Sarandon. "Hello?"

"Are you ready to make these edits?" My writing partner Pat is all business.

I mute the television. "Sure."

Actually, I'm relieved. The way that movie was shaping up, I'd probably be bawling like a calico in heat before the end of the next scene and not focusing on my work. You see, I'm a sucker for a sad movie. Some get me every single time I watch them. Take *Steel Magnolias*. I've seen it at least ten times. Don't ask me why - I'm a glutton for punishment, I guess. My eyes begin sweating, as a certain Marine calls it, along about the time that Julia Roberts goes into a coma. Then my nose stops up and tears start dripping off my chin when Sally Field, Tom Skerrit and Dylan McDermott turn off the machines keeping Julia alive. However, when Sally Field goes off on Shirley MacLaine during the funeral, I lose it - every single time.

"Why do you watch it if it's going to upset you so much," my husband asks as he fetches me a roll of toilet paper to sop up the water leaking out of my face.

"I c-c-can't help it," I blubber, blow my nose and take a sip of hot tea to clear my head.

I'm drawn to flicks that break my heart. For example, I can't stand when Chris O'Donnell gets his shoe stuck in a switch and a train runs over him in *Fried Green Tomatoes* - but I watch it over and over again anyway. Sean Penn freaking out over his lost daughter in *Mystic River* makes it hard for me to breathe. I sob when Denzel Washington is being whipped and that one tear streaks down his cheek in *Glory*. It's not the tear so much as that look of ineffable sorrow mixed with defiance. Denzel does it to me again when he says good-bye to Tom Hanks in *Philidelphia* - and Tom Hanks mourning his friend Bubba in *Forrest Gump* chokes me up too. Then there's *Terms of Endearment*, but that's a whole 'nother sob-fest.

This isn't a new development. I can remember crying over Bambi's mother and *Old Yeller* back in the days when I made my dad sit two seats over to make room for my imaginary friends, Margo and Turdibaum. Then as I grew older, there was *Jane Eyre* and *Gone with the Wind*. I broke down when Mr. Rochester's crazy wife blinded him before leaping from the ramparts to her death - and what romantic thirteen-year-old girl doesn't weep for all the lost opportunities between Rhett and Scarlet?

Then, there are those movies that I'm ashamed to admit I shed tears over - but we are friends and I'm sure you wouldn't tell anyone else that I whimpered when Kate Winslet let go of Leonardo DiCaprio's hand in *Titanic* and I wept like a baby when little **Simon Birch** died. The scene where everyone holds up either a candle or a lit Bic in **Pay It Forward** got me going too even though I knew very well that it was corny and reminiscent of **A Star is Born**.

Part of the fun of watching sad movies is to have someone with you who is crying too. My cousin Karen is a good one for that. She cries at the drop of a hat. She even emotes over scenes that I don't get like the one where Diane Keaton wails like a banshee because Jack Nicholson had a date with someone else in **Something's Gotta Give**. Stocked with plenty of popcorn and Kleenex, Karen and I spent one whole day watching the trilogy - **An Affair to Remember, The Dirty Dozen** and **Sleepless in Seattle** - because, of course, **Sleepless in Seattle** makes no sense unless you've seen the other two.

My husband cries at movies too although he pretends not to - and my son makes fun of them - and me - to keep from breaking down himself. I don't know my new daughter-in-law well enough yet, but I suspect we have a long and delicious future filled with sniveling for fun. My daughter and I do pretty well together as long as we don't look at each other. We are sophisticated film critics after all. However, if we happen to catch each other's eyes as Kevin Kline declines during **My Life As a House** or as Meryl Streep hands over her baby girl to the Nazis in **Sophie's Choice**, it's all over.

Although I tend to laugh at the idea of it, folks who bite their lips and dab their eyes at the end of emotional flicks attract me. I adore tenderhearted people - and I think it is a hopeful sign that most of us are so empathetic with the plights of others. My friend Mike told me about a television show that got to him and he had to go into a business meeting with a lump in his throat. That image moved me – and when I think about it now, I smile.

Anyway, so I avoid heartbreak with Susan Sarandon and Julia Roberts thanks to Pat's timely phone call. We finish up the project and I close my computer.

"Hey, Johnny!" I yell up the stairs.

"Yeah?"

"I'm tired of working. Let's do a movie."

"Okay. What did you have in mind?"

"There's a new one 'On Demand' called *The Notebook*. It has James Garner in it."

"Cool," he says. "Maybe it's another Maverick flick."

My Favorite Ghosts

I dig ghost movies. I love snuggling up under a quilt with the lights out, watching the shadowy phantoms flicker across the TV screen. The only thing that comes close is listening to something big sniff around the tent-stakes when you are camping out - but I digress.

Ghost stories have personality. The best ones yank our chains and make us love it. Remember that tall chick in Tevja's nightmare in *Fiddler on the Roof*? She had a hand full of keys and the longest set of beads in the history of ghost-dom. Can you imagine her rising up out of your jewelry box one day, screaming "Pearls, Keys, Pearls?" That alone would be enough to make me close my eyes and yell, "Beetlejuice, Beetlejuice, Beetlejuice!" These 'over the top' spooks are good for a laugh - although I think Beetlejuice is technically a fallen angel.

Some phantoms are sexy. Remember the one that looked like Patrick Swayze in *Ghost* - or the one that looked like Rex Harrison in *The Ghost and Mrs. Muir*? In those movies, these guys were reluctant to leave the pleasures of their earthly lives - one because he had a wife that looked like Demi Moore, the other because he had the hots for Mrs. Muir. These movies must be based on the popular Sunday school teaching that there won't be any love affairs in heaven. I presume the lustier souls among us will hold up in purgatory for an indefinite stay if that's the case.

Then there's the premise that ghosts are folks who don't know they are dead ala *The Sixth Sense* and *Poltergeist*.

Suddenly invisible, they clank around trying to get someone's attention. My high school religion teacher, Sister Imelda, would say their after-death antics are inappropriate reflections of their before death behavior. If a person was greedy, his shade might try to grab all the goodies acquired during life and 'take it with him,' so to speak. If the person was malicious, like Mary Meredith in *The Uninvited*, she might try to scare the bejesus out of anyone living in "her" house.

That poor kid in *The Sixth Sense* saw dead people all the time. How scary is that? Of course, how do we all know that we aren't seeing them too? Maybe that cranky old woman at the post office is a ghost from the 1940s who's shocked that stamps now cost thirty-nine cents. Maybe all those doctors with cold hands are "real" ghouls. Maybe those spooks from the CIA aren't just kidding around. It's a sobering thought.

Haunted critters make my skin crawl. Who can forget that red-eyed pig named Jody in *The Amityville Horror*? Or those buzzing flies all over the exorcist's face? How about that shark that kept coming back again and again in all those *JAWS* Movies? Or *Cujo*? Or those freaky lions in *The Ghost and the Darkness*? Actually, I think most cats are demons which is another category altogether and fodder for a different shriek.

Of course, Spielberg took haunted animals a big step further in *Poltergeist*. He had a haunted steak. I didn't set foot in a steakhouse for months. I still find myself poking my sirloin just to be sure it's not going to quiver on the plate.

Then there are inanimate objects - chairs that slide along the kitchen floor, closets that suck kids out of their beds, a huge assortment of macabre dolls, clowns and other toys.

There have been spectral automobiles, trains and aircraft carriers. Big old houses wreathed in fog are the norm, although The Farnsworth in Gettysburg is another manifestation. A friend of mine had an eerie coal bin in her basement. She maintained that the door closed on its own. I think it was the wind, but she preferred to be scared. I think I once had a shower in a haunted bathroom. The water turned icy and the pipes spoke to me in a deep guttural voice, "GET OUT!" I complied immediately - just in case there was a plumbing problem, of course.

eBaying at the Moon

Let's talk about eBay. What a marvelous institution! It's the electronic equivalent of Alice's restaurant – you can get whatever you want there. You can also get things you never thought possible - for example, imagine my amazement when I saw that a hardcover copy of my book, *In the Shadow of Suribachi* was for sale on eBay - considering that no hardcover copies were ever printed.

Of course, that's small potatoes in the overall history of the eBay emporium. We've all heard stories about people putting their kidneys or sperm or ova on the virtual auction block. Body part sales freak me out. I've seen *Psycho*. I've seen *Silence of the Lambs*. Who knows the ulterior motives of the bidders? If they are also browsing around for a nice chianti, trouble could be brewing.

Then there are folks who produce vaporous products of questionable reality. For example, some enterprising young man offered up his virginity to the gods of exploitation. In the first place, what makes one person's lack of sexual experience more or less valuable? If you go back to the basic principles of supply and demand, seems to me that those who are in big demand are not likely to remain virtuous for very long. Even if they remain technically "pure," I'd be willing to bet there were a few compromises along the way. On the other hand, is it likely that individuals who have had difficulty giving it away for free could draw enough of a crowd to support an auction? Given the relative interests of boys and girls, I submit that the male of the species is more likely to bid on female offerings, than the other way around. Individual tastes vary, of course.

There are some interesting eBay categories. Products listed under "Slightly Unusual" center around get-rich-quick schemes that you have to buy before you can begin getting rich. Oh there are a few oddities like plastic Jesuses and dashboard bobble boob bikini dolls, but nothing really jumps out at you.

Things take a serious step toward the wild side in "Really Weird". You can buy cans of spam to 'spam' your friends. Wow. That's really creative - not. There's also a giant bull frog in a jar up for bid. Now see, unless that bull frog's name is Kermit, it seems like you'd want to go out and collect your own amphibian. Besides, it's risky to send a pickled frog through the US Postal system. I was drawn to a CD filled with drawings of folks born with two heads and large frontal "horns." Hey, I don't make this stuff up – check it out.

After all that, I was disappointed in the "Totally Bizarre" section. After all, my physics teacher had an early version of the "amazing bobbin dunkin drinkin bird." I wasn't sufficiently intrigued to feel sentimental about it, though - and the fourteen-foot, three-D claw hammer doesn't fit in with my decor. I guess I was expecting a significant escalation in weird, but eBay must have run out of peculiar by that point. Too bad.

While I browse through eBay from time to time, I'm not patient enough for auctions. For example, I got a big kick out of the "Flip Fold" phenomenon - but I preferred to order it direct from the "Flip Fold" page. Same with all the Italian Charms I got into about a year ago. My cousin Karen acquired her charms by bidding on the ones she wanted - and then returning time and again to monitor the progress of the auction. That would have made me nuts. I want what I want when I want it. The actual act of buying isn't all that exciting for me. I'm into end results.

Having said that, who buys caskets and other funeral gear from eBay? Maybe I'm old fashioned, but I prefer to select my headstone from Monuments R Us the day before I check out - and charge it to my Mastercard. That way, my heirs can collect the frequent flyer miles.

Do You Believe in Magic?

I'm not superstitious. I'm just careful when it comes to stuff that can't be proven one way or another. I don't believe most of it for a minute – but why take chances?

When I was in school, I had an exam preparation ritual that was just this side of nutty. I'd accept the test with my left hand and position it square on my desk. Then I'd lay my pens and pencils parallel with the top the paper. A brand new pink eraser belonged one inch to the right. Then I'd take a deep breath, close my eyes and mentally address the Almighty with something like, "Please don't let me mess up." Actually, I used an earthier supplication – but you get the drift. When the teacher told us to "start", I'd breathe out in a gush of anxiety, rub my palms together and mutter to myself, "Okaaaaayyyy."

Now, I know baseball players look pretty crazy wearing the same socks all the time or jerking one ear lobe just before stepping up to bat - but how is that different from rats learning to hit the bar so they can be fed? It might not make sense to an outside observer, but if it works - it works. How do I know that my test-taking ritual was successful? I made A's. Now you might say, the A was because I knew the material. Come on. I studied hard all the time. How do you explain the time that I didn't get around to buying a fresh eraser and I ended up with an A minus? Or the time I forgot to rub my palms together and I got a B plus. The proof is in the pudding, I say.

I come by this inexplicable behavior naturally. My dad used to tell me stories about his great grandmother who was a Cherokee Indian. She could lay the palms of her hands on a table and make it levitate. When he was a little guy and got warts from handling horny toads, she'd rub the wart and it would go away. I never met the woman, but she sounded like a blast. Can you imagine her at parties? On the other hand, I'm not sure why anyone would want to levitate a table unless you dropped your napkin or something. When I pointed that out, Daddy said I was no fun.

Maybe so, but it seems to me that magic should be practical. Making elephants disappear seems like a waste of time since they are miraculous beings on the order of unicorns and satyrs. However, I can dig manna in the desert or loaves and fishes. Feeding hungry people is worth waving a wand and saying "Abracadabra" even if it does seem foolish when you think about it.

With the exception of his odd connection to a brass ball he acquired in some long ago physics class, my husband Johnny is remarkably un-superstitious. I don't know what he thinks might happen to us if he ever lets me throw the darn thing away, but I guess we all have issues that others don't appreciate. Since I'm so understanding of his neuroses, I thought he should be supportive of mine. I learned that was not to be early on in our marriage.

I've always known that red birds have the power to make wishes come true. I don't know where I got that bit of inside ornithological information but I believe its effectiveness is right up there with kissing the Blarney Stone for good luck and avoiding sidewalk cracks to support your mother's spinal health. Whenever I see a cardinal, I squeal, "There's a red bird. Make a wish." Then I close my eyes and make three wishes so that the bird in question can either choose which one of my queries to grant or if it happens to be "three-for-one" day, I'm covered. If I'm alone, I'm sure passersby avert their eyes and hurry away lest whatever I have is catching. If I'm with friends or family, they sigh and shake their heads.

Johnny and I had been married a couple days when I got up one morning and peered out the window beside our bed. "Look, look, look!" I shook him out of a sound sleep.

"What?" He smacked his lips and grunted. "Get up and take a look."

Everyone knows that you have to actually **see** the bird or the magic's no good.

He grabbed his glasses and crawled out of bed. "What am I looking for?"

I pointed. "See? Over there? In that magnolia tree?"

"A bird?"

"It's a red bird, honey."

He looked at me and raised one eyebrow. "Yeah?"

"Make a wish!" I had my wishes all laid out in my mind. Good health, good luck and long life. Those are my standards actually, but I was anxious to hear about my new husband's hopes for the future.

"I wish I had a gun." He scratched his crotch and headed for the bathroom.

Remember that handsome princes are just a wish away from horny toads.

Nate the Great

As a spectator sport, Little League rules. Outfielders disappear to answer the call of nature in the middle of the game. The third baseman sleeps at his post. The pitcher has a runny nose. The catcher sucks his thumb. The winning team gets ice cream - so does the losing team for that matter.

Back in 1980, our daughter Carmel played for a team known as the 'Reds'. Nate, our five-year-old, practiced with them. Mostly, he watched from the bench - his feet dangling, his fist lost in an enormous leather glove. Once in a while, the coach let him stand at home plate and swing the bat. Between innings, he ran the bases while I snapped pictures.

As the season waned, families took their summer vacations. For the championship game, the Reds were down several players. Then, the third baseman had to go home before the game was over.

"It's only one inning," the coach declared. "Nate can play third."

"Yeah, Nate!" I shook my fist in the air as he trotted across the field, his Nikes leaving little puffs of dust in his wake.

"NATE THE GREAT!" Carmel called from left field.

"Go, Nate!" My husband Johnny yelled through cupped hands.

The score was four to three in favor of the Reds. One short inning. The pitcher wound up. The players leaned forward.

The batter swung even though the ball was a foot over her head. Two more swings and she was out.

Nate picked his nose.

I shook a finger and mouthed, 'STOP THAT!'

He stuck out his tongue.

"Aw Jeez." Johnny nudged me. "Let him concentrate."

The next batter hit a foul ball and the catcher tagged him out. Nate made faces at his sister in the outfield.

"Nate!" I called. "Pay attention."

He wiggled his butt.

"You're distracting him," Johnny scolded.

It was down to the money. If they could make one more out, the Reds would win. The star player on the other team stepped forward. The pitch was slow. He swung from his toenails. The ball rose into the air and headed toward Nate who was tugging at his underwear.

"NATE!" The ball veered to the left.

"What?"

"Look." I pointed at the ball arcing toward him.

He glanced up.

The ball fell into his glove. THWUMP!

Shocked silence swept over the field. Nate held up the ball, grinning in wonder and delight.

The team cheered. The coach picked him up and put him on his shoulder. "NATE THE GREAT, NATE THE GREAT!" The kids chanted as they marched around the infield.

Johnny elbowed me. "Told you to leave him alone."

"Nate, zip up your jeans." I called.

Fast forward twenty-six years.

I text messaged Nate. "I just sent your wife a copy of tonight's Shriek".

"Yeah?" He answered. "Why?"

"It's called "Nate the Great."

"Aw Jeez."

It's great being a mother.

Heroes

When Alan Shepherd rocketed into history in 1961, I watched through a fuzzy black and white television brought into class by my sixth grade teacher. Too young to appreciate the adventures of Charles Lindbergh, Amelia Earhart and Jackie Cochran, I held my breath as flame spurted from the engine and the long tube eased off the launch pad. I cheered with the other kids as the helmeted, space-suited astronaut pierced the sky and then again as he arced back to earth in his tiny capsule. The combination of "daring do" and science captured my imagination and I became the greatest fan in aviation fandom. My enthusiasm lasted through high school as I followed the Mercury program into Gemini and then Apollo. In college, my fascination with the space program led me back to the beginning of aviation where I learned about the achievements of the Wright Brothers, Igor Sikorsky and Fred Weick. The idea of coming up with a concept, designing a prototype, finding money to fund it and then putting your body on the line to prove the point - that was the epitome of heroics to me.

So you can imagine my excitement when, through a friend, I received an invitation to attend the National Aviation Hall of Fame Induction Ceremony in the summer of 2001. The enshrinee list on their Web site is awash with heroes - from Eddie Rickenbacker to John Macready, Chuck Yeager to Joe Kittinger and Bob Hoover. Papa Piper is there along with the Lindberghs, Hap Arnold and Pete Conrad - the honor roll of those living and dead who pushed back the envelope of knowledge and experience. I was going to have dinner with some of these giants. Whew - I fanned myself with the invitation to fight back a sudden hot flash.

I gathered my books - *The Right Stuff, We Seven, X-15* and *Moon Shot*, fantasizing about meeting these extraordinary adventurers. I would cozy up to them and ask for their autographs. I would have my picture taken with them, grinning into the camera between the likes of John Glenn and Wally Schirra.

My husband, Johnny, is a runner-up in aviation fandom. Thrilled by this opportunity, he yielded his personal dogma of tuxedo avoidance and we drove from our home near Pittsburgh to Dayton, filled with exuberant speculations. According to our invitation, shuttle pilot Joe Engle was one of the honorees, nominated by his mentor, Chuck Yeager. That meant the ace of all aces would be there - Yeager himself - the aviation pioneer with the vision of an eagle and nerves of steel. I'd stood under "Glamorous Glennis" at the National Air and Space Museum in Washington, DC dreaming about that day in 1947 when he flew the tiny orange craft through the sound barrier. Johnny and I agreed that even a glimpse of this great hero would make it worth the long drive and overnight stay.

We arrived at the hotel just after noon. I went in to register while Johnny parked the car. I pushed through the swinging glass door and came face to face with General Yeager. Just like that. He nodded and smiled. He wasn't a giant at all. In fact, he didn't appear much taller than me and I'm five-foot-two inches tall. What's more, he was dressed in blue jeans and sneakers. I opened my mouth to introduce myself, but his focus drifted away. Grinning broadly, he hurried past me to welcome General Engle and his family who had come in behind me. I watched as they shook hands and began the good-natured banter of old friends. As much as I wanted to eavesdrop, I backed away overcome with shyness.

At the front desk, the clerk told me that our room wouldn't be ready for another half hour. Johnny came in the swinging doors as I turned around.

"Did you see him?" I mouthed.

"Who?"

"Chuck Yeager!"

"Where?"

"He and Joe Engle went out as you were coming in."

"NO!"

"Yes!"

"MAN!" Johnny spun around, squinting through the hotel windows, but the Engles and Yeager were long gone.

"What was he like?"

"Not as tall as I thought he would be."

"No way."

"Way."

While waiting for our room to open up, we rode the elevator to the top-floor restaurant. It was mid-afternoon and most of the lunch crowd had dispersed. We sat down and accepted our menus from the waiter.

"Johnny."

"What?"

"It's Scott Crossfield." I hid behind my menu.

"Where?"

"Behind you. Ten o'clock high."

"NO."

"The fastest man alive," we whispered in unison, our knees touching. I peeked around my menu. There was no mistake.

"What's he look like?" Johnny kept his voice even as if he was asking me to pass the cheese.

"Ordinary."

Johnny refused to turn around and stare even though I knew he wanted to.

"He's leaving," I whispered.

"Okay."

"He's passing behind you."

Johnny dared a quick glance over his shoulder.

"Which one?"

"The one in the golf shirt."

"No way."

"Way."

We giggled behind our fists.

After lunch, we rode the elevator downstairs to the lobby where we met our contact who introduced us to Joe Kittinger - THE Joe Kittinger. I remembered seeing his picture in Life Magazine when I was a kid. Joe parachuted out of a balloon at an altitude of 102,800 feet and was the first person to exceed the speed of sound without an airplane.

115

Thrilled, Johnny and I shook his hand. I expected someone fierce and bold, not this courtly gentleman with a dramatic gray mustache that used to be red. He, too, seemed ordinary - like the auto mechanic down the street or the guy who taught physics at the local community college.

I wanted to ask Joe what he was thinking during the nearly five minutes of free fall, but a rush to the check-in counter interrupted our conversation. The rooms were ready. I stood in line, surrounded by a plethora of octogenarians in Hawaiian shirts, shorts and sandals. I presumed that they must be aviation heroes that I didn't recognize. As I accepted my key, someone tugged at my hair, perilously close to my derrière. I whirled, ready to mow down the masher with an eloquent one liner. My jaw dropped in surprise. Three tiny old pilots grinned at me like an array of lecherous dwarves. I didn't have the heart to scold them. After all, what if they had broken a speed or altitude record fifty years ago?

"I'm not used to so many short men," I said to Johnny as we squeezed into the elevator with our luggage. "I imagined these guys would be tall and brawny. I know they are getting on in years, but they seem so little."

"Cockpits are small," Johnny said as he pressed the button. "Big men don't fit." I imagined Hulk Hogan packing himself into a Mercury space capsule and shrugged.

At seven P.M., three hours later, we found our way to the pre-ceremony cocktail party in the Aviation Hall of Fame Exhibit at Wright-Patterson Air Force Base. Weaving our way through groups of chatting pilots, we stopped at the bar to pick up our drinks.

I had discarded all plans to pursue my heroes for autographs. These fellows weren't Hollywood celebrities with stacks of eight-by-ten glossies. They were regular guys hanging out with their comrades talking about old times over a beer. Not wanting to intrude on their evening, Johnny and I decided to take in the exhibits instead. I headed toward the display area located at the far end of the hall with Johnny trailing behind me. "Excuse me," I said as I squeezed through the crowd, placing my hand on the back of a gentleman chatting with a group of admirers.

A handsome face with piercing blue eyes smiled at me. "No problem," the man said before turning back to his conversation. I gaped. Neil Armstrong. I looked at Johnny and jerked my eyes toward Neil.

"What?" Johnny cocked his head like a curious hound dog.

"Neil Armstrong." I moved my lips but made no sound. I didn't want the original moon walker to know I was gushing over him.

"Who?"

I pulled Johnny over to the side of the room.

"It's Neil Armstrong," I whispered.

"Where?"

"There." My finger shook as I pointed to one dark suit out of hundreds.

"Are you sure?"

"Yeah."

"No way."

"Way."

Dinner was in a huge room with dozens of round tables gathered around a small stage. We found our places and sat down. A beautiful woman was to my left. Her husband was the youngest pilot to fly the hump during World War II. He looked like our next door neighbor. John Glenn sat across the room on the other side of the aisle. Joe Kittinger and his pretty young wife were at a table behind us. He wore his medal around his neck on a red, white and blue ribbon. I smiled and waved to them.

Joe Foss spoke from the stage, his Medal of Honor glistening on his chest. Inductee Robin Olds was two tables over, surrounded by old drinking buddies. Neil Armstrong participated in the program, thirty-two summers after stepping off the LEM and into history. Poems and anthems supplemented the speeches. Then, suddenly, the two-hour ceremony was over. The hall was warm. Johnny was eager to get rid of the unaccustomed cummerbund. I stood up, wobbling in my high-heeled strap sandals. We bade farewell to our table mates and wound our way toward the exit. At the door, I turned for one last look.

My heroes filled the flag-festooned room with their family and friends. Uncomfortable in their fancy clothes, shy and proud in front of their loved ones, they seemed as frail and human as me. I stood there - awestruck at the magnitude of their accomplishments. They WERE ordinary. Imagine that.

Ducks, Peas and Cleavages

I'm a dreamer – no, not the pie in the sky, "I'm gonna reach the top" kind of dreamer. I mean, I go to bed at night just to enjoy the movies that flash across the screen inside my eyelids. Some are entertaining. Some are terrifying. Some are downright boring. Many are puzzling.

Sometimes my dreams have physical consequences. Once I dreamed I was stumbling down a corridor and stubbed my toe. When I woke up, there was a chip in my newly pedicured toe nail. One night I kicked Osama bin Laden and woke up with an ugly bruise on my shin. Another time, I wrestled Larry King for a peacock feather all night long and was too tired to go to work the next morning.

I often dream I'm gliding across the sky with my arms extended - and then that pleasant sensation turns to terror as I plummet into an abyss that looks like Mick Jagger's mouth - and the abyss chews me up. Shudder. Once, I awakened, sure that someone was breathing on my neck - only to find that I was still sleeping, and I couldn't tell if the wet inhalations and exhalations were real or not. I tried to scream but no sound would come out of my throat. I'm not sure if there really was no sound or if I was only dreaming there was no sound. My husband says I make all kinds of noises when I'm sleeping, so who knows?

The most horrifying nightmares were when I was a kid, and I dreamed over and over again that I was watching my grandfather sleep in a box. When I was thirteen, I thought of that dream when I stood in front of his coffin after he'd been murdered. In another one, I dreamed I was in a building that I'd designed - and it was slowly coming apart like a house of cards. I was desperate to fix it - and filled with the guilty suspicion that I'd made a mistake somewhere. I woke up with greater empathy for the designer of the Titanic.

Then there's the famous dream all students have - I wake up and realize that I've forgotten to go to class all semester long - and now I have to take a test and I don't have a clue what the class was about. Or the alternative terror, I dream I wake up to discover I'm late for a test, but I'm not sure if I'm awake and it's really late or if I'm still asleep dreaming that it's late. The last time I went to school that it mattered was more than fifteen years ago, but I still have those dad-gummed dreams.

I also have the one where my teeth are soft and all there is to eat is steak. And the one where I'm wearing a low-cut dress and the legs of the chair I'm sitting on are made of PlayDoh and I'm slowly sinking into the floor and the man sitting next to me (who looks just like Rush Limbaugh) is towering higher and higher over me - and every time he looks down, he drops peas into my cleavage. Or the one where there is a snake living in the toilet and it comes out at night and I can hear its scales scraping across the tile floor - and then suddenly the shower comes on. Or the one where a wolf who lives under my bed reads *To Kill a Mockingbird* in a gruff snarling tone that keeps me awake all night.

Sometimes other people's dreams are stranger than my own. For example, my daughter says that she dreams that she's careening down a highway and none of the controls on the car work. My husband dreams that he's backing a Volvo down an endless mountain trail - without brakes. I maintain that that's how he drives anyway - but that's a different shriek. Years ago, when we were dating, he entertained me for an evening telling me about how he dreamed he was a duck. He denies it now. Every once in a while, I think he might really have been a duck in an earlier life. He denies that too.

There are times I can't sleep for fear the wolf under the bed will go after the duck snoring beside me. Or was that something I dreamed while on Tylenol PM?

Hugs

It was a beautiful day in Branson, Missouri. We were there early. I sat in a corner waiting for the miracle that was about to happen. Seven soldiers in their seventies were coming together after more than fifty years. They had been mere boys when last they'd seen each other. Captured by the North Koreans in 1950, they had marched hundreds of miles – ever wary of guards urging them along with bayonet pricks and gunfire. Together with nearly two hundred other American prisoners, they boarded a railway car at the behest of their captors. The train ended up in a long dark tunnel. Over a two-day period, the men in each boxcar were taken out and massacred. Only twenty lived to tell about the bodies sprawled along the railroad tracks.

Time has taken all but eight. Over the last year, through coincidence and design, the survivors of the Sunchon Tunnel Massacre found each other again. Although one man was too ill to make the journey, seven decided to get together - to compare notes, to share, to wonder at life's blessings. I'd been invited to attend - an honor I'll not soon forget. As the clock chugged toward the appointed time, I wondered at the courage it takes to choose life after what these men had gone through. What dreams fill their sleep? Does joy taste differently after such horror?

They entered the hotel lobby one at a time. Some had their wives with them. Some brought grandchildren. Some carried themselves with the air of much younger men. Others leaned on walkers or canes. Most wore caps identifying them as ex-

POWs. They greeted each other with wide grins and hearty back slaps. "I'd recognize you anywhere," one said to another. "All these years, I thought you'd died," another murmured as he embraced an old comrade.

After a few minutes, the men realized that the rest of us were there. I stood up - shaking hands at first - and then I was scooped into the arms of a ghost - and then another and another. As the weekend progressed, it became clear that other forms of human communication just didn't work under these circumstances. We hugged each other, the limo driver and his wife, the members of the Branson Veteran's Task force who arranged the event, waitresses, entertainers, reporters - and casual passers-by. We hugged when we were having our pictures made. We hugged when someone told a sad story - and when the story was funny. We hugged when words got stuck in our throats. We hugged instead of crying. We spaced our meetings to include hugging time. We hugged when we said hello and when we said good-bye.

I learned many things this past week - that tragic events don't change you but merely intensify who you already are, that love is as complicated as life - and that you have to work at being happy every day. And these men - Ed, Bill, Val, Bob, Walt, Jim and Sherm - taught me the value of a simple hug. Thank you for that, guys - and everything else.

Guilt

Dogs and babies are masters of the proverbial 'guilt trip'. Peanut is a three-pound poodle who sniffs her owner's breath. If she detects ice cream, she searches for her share. If the treat isn't delivered post haste, she curls up with her chin on her paws and whimpers in dismay. Personally, I'd rather walk through fire than disappoint Peanut. Kids are worse. When my son Nate was a baby, he was the master of the quivering lower lip, which was so cute and so pitiful that no parent or grandparent could deny him whatever it was he was trying to con out of us.

Yep. Guilt works. It's the guiding principle behind creative whining which I've used successfully for many years. Of course, it's not always easy. Often there's a duel between two competing parties intent on scoring a decisive blow and rendering the other helpless and culpable.

Here's how it goes. My car dies. I go to a mechanic named Mel. I know his name is Mel because "Mel" is embroidered on his baseball cap. He is sitting in his tiny office reading "Playboy" and eating a tuna fish sandwich. He scores the first point because I feel guilty intruding on his lunch break. However, it's 10:30 A.M. The shop didn't open until 10:00. I'm quite sure that he's not going to starve to death any time soon - nor will his tuna get cold while I share my problem with him. I suck it up and explain about the odd sound my car is making.

Mel swallows a great mouthful of tuna and postulates that my infarculator is broken. I remind him that he fixed it only a few months ago - and smile, asking if there has been an infarculator recall and I just didn't get my notice in the mail. He says there have been no infarculator recalls - but he can't meet my eyes. I know without a doubt that there's something fishy about my infarculator problem.

"Can you fix it?"

He eyes the ceiling and scratches his chin. "Nope."

I say, "How soon before you can replace it?"

"Next week."

"Why does it take so long?"

"Have to order the part."

I see a vast storeroom behind him filled to the ceiling with shelves of boxes labeled "infarculators." Infarculator kits hang from peg boards. There's a whole wall of Acura TL infarculators over by the water cooler. In fact, there is a patch affixed over the chest pocket on his coveralls that says, "Infarculators R Us."

I have several choices. I can throw a fit. It's tempting - but in the end, I might feel guilty - and of course, that means Mel wins. I could walk away and find another infarculator repairman - but I don't like the feel of that approach. It seems too much like caving which is the same as losing. Malicious deceit is an option, but in the end, I go for creative whining.

I wring my hands. "What am I going to do? I have to drive to Columbus to give blood to twenty-eight Iberian orphans just in from Lamborghini."

Okay, so I stretched the truth a bit. I don't know anyone from Lamborghini.

"Is that so? I sure hate to hear about those bloodless orphaned Iberians. Seems like there's hard luck everywhere I look," Mel says. "Why just this morning I got an email from some fellow in Africa whose parents were killed in a car crash. Wanted me to help him out. Was willing to pay me a pretty penny for my time."

Hmm. If he's serious, he's being scammed by one of the biggest phishing ploys around - and I should feel guilty for trying to guilt out such a guileless soul. If he's kidding me, he's a master of the sport and I'm likely to get creamed in the next round.

I'm furious, but I put on my mildest, most sincere face. "Do you think I can make it to Columbus? Those kids are waiting for me."

He looks startled. "I wouldn't drive that car five miles."

I lay my hand on his forearm. "What should I do?"

He pauses.

I let my eyes fill with tears.

"Well, I **could** make a few phone calls."

"Could you?"

"Send my brother down to the warehouse."

I look at my watch. "Those poor kids are expecting me."

"Things just don't get done that fast around here, Missy. I have other customers ahead of you."

There's not another soul in the shop. No other cars either. I let a tear roll partway down my cheek before I wipe it away with the back of my hand.

127

"Well, I'm sure Dan Weatherman can wait on **his** infarculator."

"How soon?"

"How about two?"

Okay, so anyone else would be thrilled when the time it takes to replace an infarculator goes from a week to three and a half hours - but now I know that it can be done in three and a half hours, I'm quite sure I'm still being milked for labor costs. Let's see. He has to drive the car into his garage. Put it up on a lift. Unbolt old infarculator. Bolt in new infarculator. Test infarculator. Lower lift. Drive car out of garage. Write up ticket. Hand me back my keys. Mentally I figure thirty minutes tops.

Argh!

I take a deep shuddering breath. "I need to get started long before then." (Notice I didn't say get started on what.)

"You got me at a disadvantage here, ma'am. There's only so much a man can do."

I dig a handkerchief out of my purse and dab my eyes. "I promised." (I thought about wailing, but decided that might be too much.)

He melts and I know I have him. "Maybe I can use a rebuilt infarculator I have here in the shop."

"How long would **that** take?"

"I'll have you out of here in an hour."

I frown.

"Forty-five minutes if I get started right now."

"Thank you, thank you, thank you."

A half hour later, I drive away happy - my car is fixed and I won the guilt-out. Life is good.

At lunch over chocolate fudge cake at SoHo, I give a girlfriend the run-down on my spectacular win.

"You mean you took advantage of a working man?" Her eyes are large and accusing.

"It was him or me."

"He probably has a wife and children to support."

I stick out my lower lip. "He got paid handsomely for his few minutes work."

"But you **lied** to him, Joyce."

"No, I didn't. I let him draw his own conclusions."

"You mean there **are** Iberian children waiting for blood transfusions in Columbus?"

I duck my chin and mumble under my breath, "No, there are no Iberian children."

"And there's no Lamborghini either, right?"

"No, no Lamborghini."

"I see," she says and stares at our shared dessert.

Shame flushes my cheeks bright red and the sweet concoction turns bitter in my mouth. I lay down my fork.

She polishes off the last of the ganache and whipped cream, looks up and smiles. "Mmmm."

She's better than my mother at the guilt game.

129

The Phantom of Bob Evans

I got to Bob Evans around 12:30 right in the middle of the lunchtime crowd. The hostess was a friendly soul. She escorted me to a big booth in the front. I scooted in and ordered a diet cola. While the waitress collected it, I examined the menu. "I want two eggs over medium," I told her.

She scratched on her paper pad. "And two pieces of bacon well-done but not too well-done."

I'd eaten lunch there before.

While my meal was cooking, I read my email. By the time the waitress set my plate in front of me, I'd already put together a to-do list, made an appointment with another writer and began reading a manuscript. As I finished eating, I felt someone looking at me. I glanced around. The bus boy smirked and avoided my eyes. The women behind the counter winked. Hmm. I smiled and went back to my book.

A minute later, my waitress slid into the booth across the table from me. "You know that man that was sitting over there?" She pointed.

The restaurant was half-empty now. I didn't remember anyone sitting at that table. "No."

She suppressed a giggle and wadded up my bill, which was stuck under the honey bottle. "He bought your lunch because you look like his old girlfriend."

"What? Me?" I spun my head around.

"He's gone now." She folded her arms over her chest and grinned.

I opened my mouth a couple of times like a panting guppie. "Cool," I finally managed. I left, shaking my head and wondering why anyone would do such a thing.

My husband laughed when I told him. "Maybe I should hang out at Morton's and see if some chick will buy my lunch because I look like an old boyfriend."

Yeah, yeah, yeah.

A few minutes later, I emailed my poet-friend Carolyn. "Awww," she answered. "It was his good deed for the day. He probably felt sorry for you, that you were so busy that you couldn't taste what you were eating anyway."

Yeah, I thought. That's it. He must be a person with a good heart.

"I just love when that happens," my daughter-in-law chuckled when I told her.

"How odd!" was my son's response.

Hmm, I thought. Does it happen a lot? I've had men buy me drinks at a bar and send them to me with a flourish. They want to - er - get to know me better - but this fellow didn't seem to want a thing.

"Maybe he was impotent," my straight-shooting-philosophical-friend Alan opined. "Or really ugly. Sort of a Phantom-of-the-Opera kind of guy."

I visualized a man with a white half-mask eating pancakes at Bob Evans. Naw. I wasn't so busy that I would miss someone like that.

"Maybe he's a serial killer," my suspicious-chocoholic-friend Anna Marie said over dinner at the Olive Garden. "Maybe he's going to stalk you."

That was an ugly thought.

"Maybe he followed you here and is going to buy your dinner too," she continued.

I glanced over my shoulder. An elderly couple was eating lasagna behind me. They didn't look too scary.

"Maybe this time he'll buy dessert," Anna Marie said as she perused the menu for any chocolate options in case my benefactor actually showed up with wallet in hand.

The whole serial-killer-dessert-buyer scenario didn't go over with my romantic-creative-writer-friend Kathe. "He must still have a crush on that ex-girlfriend," she emailed me. "She must have been the one to break it off and he's still pining."

Awww. I felt bad that this poor stranger bought my lunch in honor of a woman who broke his heart.

"Was it your red hair (an immediately notable feature) or the fact that you were working during your meal (behavior-driven recognition) or (this is the most intriguing) is he actually an old boyfriend?" Kathe pondered electronically.

Hmm. I closed her email and considered all my old boyfriends. It didn't seem likely that I would walk into a restaurant and not see someone that I knew - unless he'd changed a lot in the intervening years. On top of that, I couldn't imagine how a man who'd been my boyfriend forty years ago back in Ft. Smith, Arkansas would just happen to be eating breakfast at my local Bob Evans in Bridgeville, Pennsylvania - and that he would recognize me.

"How about this," my practical-joker-friend Chris proposed. "What if someone you know was playing you?"

"Playing me?"

"You know, calling the restaurant and setting you up?"

"Setting me up for what?"

"Lunch?"

Okay, so that seemed pretty far-fetched.

"Maybe it was someone paying it forward?" My young-movie-addict-friend Bobby suggested.

"I didn't see anyone that looked like Kevin Spacey."

"You didn't see anyone at all."

I couldn't argue with that. "So what am I supposed to do?"

"Do something nice for someone else."

"Like what?"

"Like give a poor homeless fellow on the street a hamburger."

"I do that sometimes anyway."

"Well, that's it then, silly. You are getting paid back."

That didn't seem right. If it was really some karmic justice kind of thing then the good deed should go to someone who couldn't afford lunch at Bob Evans - not me.

"It's a secret admirer," my journalist-friend Tom insisted. "And he wants you to notice him."

"He didn't stick around to be noticed."

"I don't know about that," Tom said. "Seems to me that if I wanted to get a woman to think about me, I'd do something that would make her wonder."

Hmm. Well, if that's the case, it certainly worked. I wondered about that summertime Santa all day long – but then, as I was getting ready for bed, it dawned on me. It didn't matter who he was or what his motivations were. What mattered is that in a horn-honking, impatient, frustrating world - someone was good to me - for no real reason. Hallelujah!

Once Upon a Time . . .

The coffee shop lights were dim. I could not make out the faces of the folks sitting in the far corner. I opened my book and thumbed to a short story titled, "Andrew". It is one of my favorites. It is about two soldiers whose paths crossed in the wilderness as they found their way home after the Civil War. It is about dealing with having killed - and it is about dealing with your own approaching death. Those are risky subjects for a writer – but for once, I nailed it. At least, I thought so.

I cleared my throat and began.

Two young girls sipped their lattes and pretended to be interested. It was nice of them, but they were used to *The Simpsons* and *Superman* movies. I turned the page. When I got to the part where Grover accidentally shoots Andrew, a lady to my left set her coffee cup down and leaned her chin on her fist. Towards the middle of the story, a middle-aged man in biker leathers nodded knowingly. At the end of the reading, there was a long moment of silence as the audience pondered the meaning of the last line - or maybe they were waiting to see if I was finished. The applause was warm. I wasn't sure if they liked "Andrew" - or me. Or if they were just being polite.

The lights were turned up and I saw that there were more people in the room than I realized. The teen-aged girls approached me with notebooks in hand. One was a poet - the other was working on a novel. I had misread them. We talked about writing and I gave each of them my business card.

When they left, a gaunt gray woman emerged from the shadows. She had my book tucked under her arm. "Very moving," she rasped. "Poignant." I thanked her and offered her a card. She shook her head. "I've got your number." She went outside to smoke a cigarette. Puzzled, I watched her through the glass door. It was cold and she didn't wear a coat. She squinted into the frigid wind before she lit up and I fancied, for a moment, that I could see the bones beneath her skin. I shuddered and looked away.

"Can I talk to you?"

His face was inches from mine. I jumped.

"I didn't mean to scare you." The old man leaned on his walker. "I need to talk to you."

"Of course. What can I do for you?"

"Let me buy you a cup of coffee?"

I nodded and sat down at a tall round table while the old man ordered and brought me my mug. He settled beside me.

"I liked your story."

"Thank you. Are you a writer too?"

"I am – but nothing like you." He blew across the rim of his coffee cup and I smelled winter on his breath.

Spooked, I waited as he searched for words.

"I have a story," he said finally. "I've tried to write it for sixty-three years."

"Maybe you are trying too hard?"

"Maybe." He lowered his head.

I lost track of everyone else in the room, hypnotized by the tears frozen on his cheeks.

"Time is running out - and I still can't do it."

I sat quietly - listening.

"Tonight, when you were reading your story, I knew that you were the one."

"The one?"

"The one to write this story."

"You mean you want me to be your ghost?"

"No. I'm not asking you to write under my name. I'm going to give you the story. No strings. You can write it anyway you want."

"Why?"

"Because you are the only way I can save an old friend."

I sipped my coffee. "You want to tell me about it?"

"When I was a boy, I had a buddy. He was like a brother." His voice dropped to a near-whisper.

I leaned forward.

The old man's memories were glossy pearls reflecting the soul of a boy who died on a distant battlefield long before I was born. His words sketched a face. My own imagination colored it. When he was done, the old man reached across the table and covered my hand with his cool one. "You will write about him?"

"I promise."

He seemed comforted. "I don't want him to disappear when I do."

"I understand."

He stood up and put on his coat.

"They are going to read more poems tonight," I said.

"I'm finished." He pointed towards the door. The gaunt woman on the other side of the glass beckoned. "She's waiting for me."

I watched him shuffle toward the door using his walker. A bell tinkled and cold air gushed in as he went out. The woman snuffed out her cigarette and embraced him. I turned back to my coffee.

The business card I had given him lay on the table. I picked it up and turned to call him, but they were already gone.

"Did you have fun," my husband asked when I called later that night.

I told him about the old man and his story.

"Will you write about it?"

"Someday."

"What is this? The millionth story someone has given you? You should turn your collar around and put out a shingle."

I laughed. "I'm the glue."

Now he was laughing. "Glue?"

"Story tellers are the glue between people who lived before and those who live now - and those who will live in the future."

He was quiet for a while. "It's a big responsibility, Joyce."

"No, it's a blessing."

Other books by Joyce Faulkner
available from www.RedEnginePress.com or
www.Amazon.com.

In the Shadow of Suribachi is stories of young men whose lives are forever changed in the battle for Iwo Jima.

ISBN: 978-0-9745652-0-0

$15.95 USD

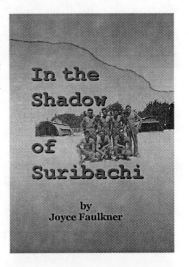

Losing Patience is a collection of short stories with revealing character and surprises.

ISBN: 978-0-9745652-4-8

$15.95 USD

Greeting cards featuring the illustrations found in this book are available from www.RedEnginePress.com.

Joyce Faulkner is a Pittsburgh based freelance writer, columnist and author. Her novel, *In the Shadow of Suribachi*, received the 2006 Military Writers Society of America Gold Medal for Historical Fiction. She is a member of the Audio Divas, a group of women who produce CDs and speak around the country on topics of interest to writers. *For Shrieking Out Loud!* is based on her column for TheCelebrityCafe.com, known as "The Weekly Shriek."

Kathe Gogolewski has worked as a professional muralist, caricaturist and dance theater artist for over twenty years. Recently, she has designed and painted murals throughout San Diego, California, including several in the oncology unit at Children's Hospital. She has designed costumes, props and backdrops for the Lamorinda Ballet Company in Moraga, California. Kathe has authored a young readers book, *Tato*.

Printed in the United States
89199LV00002B/397-444/A